Out-lanta
A Second Chance Novella
Magnolias and Moonshine Novella Book 13

Tina DeSalvo

Also by Tina DeSalvo

Elli, a Second Chance Novel
Jewell, a Second Chance Novel
Hunt for Christmas, a Second Chance Novella
And coming Summer 2017 - Abby, a Second Chance Novel

"Tina DeSalvo writes with warmth and wit. Her characters leap off the page into your heart!" – *Cherry Adair, NY Times Bestselling Author*
"Elli is...a delightful and uplifting read...it's simply excellent in so many ways! A keeper." – *NY Times Bestselling Author, Heather Graham*
"Tender, tense, a sweet yet sexy love story. In Jewel, Tina DeSalvo takes us inside our deep fears and fantasies in a tale as poignant as it is innovative and satisfying." – *Stella Cameron, New York Times Bestselling Author of the Alex Duggins Mysteries.*

What readers are saying about Tina's books...

"Hunt for Christmas, a Second Chance Novel, by Tina DeSalvo is the perfect holiday read. Or anytime read, for that matter. It's sweet and sexy with a large helping of smolder."

"An adorable Cajun Christmas romance novella. Touching and smart. A sweet read to lift your spirits for an afternoon break."

Jewell was an amazingly dynamic character to follow around who's lessons and experiences could teach readers about some of the themes that apply to their own lives. This story has all of the perfect elements that makes a page turning session into late nights of obsessive reading."

"This book is amazing!!!"

"Jewell is full of mystery, romance, family matters, and a grand plantation with some secrets."

"The kind of story that pulls you in and doesn't let you go. You end each chapter eager to start the next and are sorry when the last chapter ends."

This book was fun to write, thanks to the lovely people who knew so much more than I do about Polish food, culture and language. You know who you are...I wish I could name each of you. Please know how grateful I am to you for your inspiration and knowledge. This Italian-American girl living in Cajun country would never have been able to understand *Chruscki, dill pickle soup,* and *the Polish Babcia* if it wasn't for you. I hope I captured the wonderful spirit that resides in you...in Ania, as she experiences the deep south of the US for the first time.

Welcome to the Magnolias and Moonshine series, where you'll fall in love with the South.

Twenty New York Times, USA Today, and Amazon bestselling authors joined together to bring you a taste of Southern charm in this brand-new Magnolias & Moonshine series.

There is something for everyone with these ten sweet and ten sizzle contemporary romance novellas. You'll enjoy stories with cowboys, weddings, county fairs, lovers reunited, and much more.

Step into the world of the South and hear the cicadas, taste the mint juleps, see the stars, and smell the magnolias.

Authors in novella release order:

Ciara Knight (Sweet)

Hildie McQueen (Sizzle)

Beth Williamson (Sizzle)

Susan Hatler (Sweet)

Lindi Peterson (Sweet)

Kymber Morgan (Sizzle)

Amanda McIntyre (Sizzle)

Lucy McConnell (Sweet)

Sharon Hamilton (Sizzle)

Lisa Kessler (Sizzle)

Kirsten Osbourne (Sweet)

Susan Carlisle (Sizzle)

Tina DeSalvo (Sizzle)

Raine English (Sweet)

Amelia C. Adams (Sweet)

E. E. Burke (Sizzle)

Melinda Curtis (Sweet)

Merry Farmer (Sizzle)

Shanna Hatfield (Sweet)

Jennifer Peel (Sweet)

Chapter One

"Okay ladies, I'm all yours," Luke Marcelle said as he climbed into his sleek, deep red BMW M3 convertible. He'd left the Jeep he used for work back home in Louisiana, choosing to make the road trip to Atlanta in what he called his recreational vehicle. Luke put his Nikon digital camera into his backpack on the center console between the front seats. He turned to look at his passengers in the back seat. "I got my photos from the beautiful Swan House and boxwood gardens for work. I'm finished here at the Atlanta History Center. The rest of the afternoon is for your pleasure."

"And we are here for youz pleasure, too," eighty-eight-year-old Izzy Bienvenu said from the back seat where she sat under an enormous floppy straw hat to the right of her fifty-something year old niece, Ruby. Both women were from Cane, Louisiana where Luke had moved his business a few years ago. "It's nice we'ze all happened to be in Atlanta at da same time. We'ze are ready to party wit you and take youz mind off of work."

Tanté Izzy and Ruby looked like they were ready for a NFL Sunday game in the the Superdome rather than 'partying' in the springtime with him. Luke appreciated their team loyalty and got a chuckle seeing them in their bedazzled black and gold New Orleans Saints t-shirts and huge black, sunglasses that looked like bumblebee eyes. Even though football season was months away, Tanté Izzy said they were wearing the Saint's t-shirts because they wanted the Atlanta Falcon fans to know that their rival Who-Dat fans were around. She sure enjoyed making the sport of fan-mania an all year long fandom. The fancy sunglasses they wore had nothing to do with being a super-fan, though. According to Tanté Izzy she and ruby wore them because they looked sexier with them on in while riding in his red-hot convertible with the top down.

"Party?" Ruby said, shaking her head, causing her bright red bangs to swish across her forehead from under the giant hat she wore. "Don't you think that's an overstatement. Luke here doesn't want to go out dancing and clubbing with us, Tanté Izzy. He's too busy for that. He's just going to spend an afternoon with us. Remember, he's got a lot to do for that big project he's bidding on. It's for that new neighborhood that he wants to build not too far from Cane. The one he's taking all those pretty pictures for." She looked at Luke. "What's it called again?"

"Magnolia Row."

"He's going to grow his construction company from building houses and commercial buildings one client at a time to building thousands of houses for just one client." Ruby explained to Tante' Izzy who was adjusting her own huge hat on her tiny head.

"He hasn't gotten dat big job, yet," Tanté Izzy whispered to Ruby, but he heard her just fine from the front seat. "He's still got to win da bid over two other companies. We'ze here to take his mind off of dat. So hush youz mouth." Then in a louder voice she spoke directly to Luke. "Ruby and I are ready to go on da Walking Dead Tour."

"From the Classical 1928 Swan House, or as you ladies refer to it as President Snow's Mansion from The Hunger Games to the Walking Dead tour." He started the car and closed his eyes, enjoying the sound of the powerful engine purring to life. Just then, the passenger door flung open and a rustle of noisy fabric and feathers along with a blur of bright white filled the front seat.

"What the hell?" Either he was hallucinating or a beautiful dark haired bride had just jumped in his car.

"Go, Go, Go," the stranger in white screamed, banging on the dash. Even though she'd only spoken three short words, he could tell she had a foreign accent. The bride looked past him with big blue eyes focused on the woodland path on the other side of the parking lot.

"Drive! Please."

"Hell no. I've seen this movie and I'm not interested in Buford T. Justice chasing me across Georgia."

"Oh. I get out then if you do not drive." The woman started to shift to get out of the car, struggling with the dress. The top of the dress fit like plastic wrap on her very shapely body making it difficult for her to bend and move. Yet, as stingy that part of her dress was with fabric, the bottom more than compensated for it. Starting with a huge flare around her knees, there seemed to be miles of voluminous fabric there. It equally made movement a problem for her. How had she even managed to get into his sports car?

She looked somewhere past him again.

"No. He drive," Ruby said, unintentionally speaking like the runaway bride had.

"Yes?" she asked, her voice shaky one second and in the next her hand flew to her mouth and she shouted with complete assertiveness. "I need you driving. Now. They are coming. Hurry." Her accent was heavier than it was at first. She was now adding a "k" at the end of her ing words.

"Go. Go. Go." Tanté Izzy and Ruby screamed at the same time.

"One of those three men wearing the tuxedoes, has a gun," Ruby shouted. "God, he must be the jilted groom."

"I gotz my gun too," Tanté Izzy yelled, reaching into her purse. Hearing that was all the incentive Luke needed. The thought of a shoot-out between an angry fiancé and an elderly Cajun woman had him punching his foot on the accelerator. The powerful engine responded as it was engineered to and they sped off.

The bride's veil blew up behind her like a kite tail, whipping Tanté Izzy and Ruby in the face as it trailed onto the back.

"Oh, no," the bride cried, tugging on the material flying behind her head. It caught the wind and came around to cover Luke's face. He slammed on his brakes.

"Are you trying to get us killed?" he yanked the white fabric off of his face as she tried bundling it up into a ball. That's when a ping sounded near the side of the car. All three women screamed.

Luke flinched and floored it. "Holy crap, lady. I've heard of shotgun weddings before, but this is ridiculous."

"Oh, God, I'm going to be dead," she said, folding over onto her lap and giving Luke a full view of the back of her dress and the deep plunge which left a view of more fair skin than not. Hell, there was hardly any dress in the back at all.

"I'm calling 9-1-1," Ruby shouted. "A person should be able to say no and leave a wedding if they want...even the bride."

"*Nie*. No. Please." The woman jerked up, reached around and grabbed the phone from Ruby's hand. A tear slid down her cheek. "No police. I get out of car," she offered and looked back to see if anyone was following them.

Luke did the same. Two cars cut the corner behind them. He sped up and took the next turn and then three after that without slowing down. His car was a performance dream. The women were grabbing onto the back and bottom of their seats to keep from falling over, even though the car hugged each turn smoothly. Luke hooked a hard, fast left and pulled into what looked like an old office parking garage. He hit the brakes, turned the wheel and stopped the car facing in the direction they had just come it. He turned off the headlights and the darkness from the empty garage closed in around them. He left the engine running.

"Where can I drop you off?" he asked the woman with the white knuckled grip on his dash.

Tanté Izzy smacked him in the back of the head and leaned between the console seats. "You liked drivin' fast too much."

"Hey, I was just trying to keep us from getting shot."

"You are crazy driver," the bride said, letting go of the dash. "Thank you for keeping us not getting dead."

"Youz talk funny. Where are youz from?"

The woman looked over her shoulder to Tanté Izzy, then back toward where cars were passing on the street outside of the parking garage. "Lithuania," she replied, but something in her tone told Luke she was lying. "You have an accent too. Where are you from?"

"God's country." Tanté Izzy said with a big smile. Ruby nodded next to her.

"That's for sure," Ruby added. "We're from a town called Cane in Louisiana. It's near New Orleans."

"Ruby and I is Cajun," Tanté Izzy piped in, as if that explained everything. "Luke's not Cajun by birth but he'z Cajun by friendship."

The probably not-Lithuanian bride's dark brows lifted. She clearly didn't understand what any of that meant, but didn't ask for an explanation. She was looking around the quiet parking garage.

Luke pulled out his phone. "Shall I call you a cab?"

"No. I can walk." She picked Ruby's phone up off the floor where it had fallen in the mad getaway dash, and handed it back. "I'm sorry for taking it." Luke frowned hearing her insert a k again in an *ing* word - to make taking sound like *takink*. Her accent made her sound more vulnerable somehow. She opened the door, the bottom of her wedding dress poured out like a flooding river over the banks.

"No. Don't go," Ruby said, squeezing her broad shoulders into the small space next to Tanté Izzy so she could get closer to the bride. "It's not safe for you to walk through the streets with an angry fiancé and his posse of groomsmen chasing after you. Not to mention that it will be impossible to drag that long Cathedral train behind you." Ruby lowered her sunglasses down her nose and looked over the top of them. "From what I can see—spilling out the door like that—it sure looks like a real pretty train."

"We'ze ain't goin' to throw her to da wolves." Tanté Izzy said looking at Luke.

He shook his head. "You must have friends or family you can call."

She sighed. "I can walk."

Oh hell. That wasn't the response he wanted to hear. Luke grabbed the steering wheel and looked out his window into the dark, dusty garage.

"Luke Marcelle," Tanté Izzy said, "dis girl needs our help and we'ze goin' to give it to her. Don't make her feel bad about it either. It took a lot of courage to walk out of her own wedding when all da people came to wish her a happy life."

The woman looked at Tanté Izzy. "You are a good *Babcia*. I thank you but I don't want trouble for you or your grandson and daughter."

"Dey aren't my grandson and daughter," Tanté Izzy corrected. "Dey are family, Ruby by blood and Luke by friendship. Dey also are da peoples who are gonna help you."

Chapter Two

"Thank you, *Babcia*." Relief mingled with fear made Ania Darska's body feel cold, although the air was warm and still. She'd gotten a break, if for only a short time.

"I like you callin' me *Babcia*," Tanté Izzy said, her cloudy green eyes softening. "I don't know what it means, but it sounds like a nice word. My name is Tanté Izzy." The old lady pushed back the huge brim of her huge hat, then patted Ania on her bare shoulder. Her fingers were thin, firm. The gentle touch made her think of her own grandmother whose hard working hands felt the same when she'd touched her as child back in Poland.

"Babcia—it means grandmother."

Ania could feel the small round medal of the iconic painting of the Black Madonna and child, biting into her big toe where it had settled in her left shoe. Her mother, God rest her soul, would be surprised and mortified that Ania had stepped on the special protective medal she had given her only daughter. She wouldn't be surprised, however, that it was now causing Ania such discomfort and guilt. Her mother would have said that was because the Madonna-Queen of Poland-as disappointed that Ania had claimed she was from Lithuania, not her beautiful homeland of Poland.

Ania felt terrible lying to these nice people who'd nearly been shot because of her. She hated not telling them why she had run from her wedding too. These were good, normal people. People who didn't carry their only possession in the world inside a crystal-adorned pump. If they knew she had been about to marry a cold-blooded killer for the Polish-American mob, then they would call the police and expose her to a horrible fate she hoped to avoid. It would make no difference for them to know that she was to marry this killer only because she had no other choice.

She and her blessed medal of the Lady of Czestochowa had to get out of town and hide. To do that, Ania had to...what? God, she didn't have a clue. Her options were limited. She had no money, no car, no family, no friends, no passport.

Turning, she looked at the two women in the back seat who were her only allies for now. She avoided making eye contact with the very tall, dark haired man with the broad shoulders and the piercing hazel eyes. They had called him Luke. He did not trust her. She understood that. She was a stranger with a groom who'd tried to shoot him. This Luke frightened her, even though he couldn't be that bad of man if he was with the two nice ladies in the back seat. Still, he was a strong, fit, muscular man. In the last few years, all of the men she'd met whose muscles pulled tight against their shirts as Luke's did in his pale blue button down shirt, were dangerous.

Luke was looking at her like she had two alien heads and a spiked tail. He wanted her to leave. She needed to go. She had to figure out how to do that and stay away from Dorek.

"She doesn't look like she heard your question, Tanté Izzy," the red-hair woman named Ruby said. What question? Ania hadn't heard it. Ruby smiled at her and it confirmed what Ania already believed of the middle-aged woman by her friendly gestures and soft expressions. She was a pleasant person. It made her feel bad again that she had dragged them all into all of this. "Ask her again. I think she's in shock," Ruby told Tanté Izzy.

Ask me what? Am I in shock?

"This is insane," Luke, said, frowning. He was clearly annoyed with her, or with the situation, or both. She slid as far away from him as possible as he looked at her again with his piercing eyes. He ran his hand through his nearly black wavy hair, then opened the console between them and pulled out bottles of water until everyone had one. It was cold. How did the water stay cold in the console in his car? Was the console an ice chest?

"What's your name?" Tanté Izzy asked, her gentle voice in contrast to Luke's harsher one.

"Ania." She opened her water but didn't drink. "My name is Ania...Mitchell."

"Yeah? Mitchell. That sounds like a Lithuanian name if I ever heard one." Luke took a long drink of his water.

"It is a name from England," she said, not thinking before she spoke. "There were some English people who settled in Lithuania, a long time ago." Dear Lord, what was she saying? Ania wiggled her toe against the Black Madonna medal.

When had she become such a liar?

When Dorek and his father decided they wanted her dead.

"Very long ago," she continued when he looked at her as if she'd grown a third head. "Lithuania had a lot of foreigners at one time. Latvia borders it to the north, Belarus to the east and Poland to the south..."

"...and England is twelve-hundred miles or more to the west." Luke shook his head, recapped his water and put the empty bottle back into the console.

"Really? Your ancestors had to travel far to settle in Lithuania," Ruby said, earning a groan from Luke.

Ania took a sip of the water, finding it hard to swallow past the panic lodged in her throat. Luke knew she was lying. What would he do about it?

"I can walk," she managed after taking another sip of water. She put the water bottle in the drink holder and stepped out of the car.

Mitchell was a good name, and she was pleased that her panicked brain could come up with a false name so quickly. Ania loved Margaret Mitchell and the one novel she wrote from her apartment that wasn't very far from where they were parked right now. *Gone with the Wind* was a survivor's story. Margaret Mitchell had a personal survivor's story too. She had written the coming of age story of Scarlett O'Hara trying to survive the ravages of war while recovering from injuries she received in a car-crash. Mitchell had to survive other injuries too. She had three automobile accidents, two falls from horseback, severe burns when her clothes caught fire, and even a concussion when she was hit in the head by a bottle of whiskey that was thrown by a drunken guest at a party she was attending. Margaret Mitchell had been a survivor.

And so was she. She related to the author in her own, odd way having been knocked down over and over again.

"So where do you intend to walk to?" Ruby asked, standing inside the car. "Oh, standing feels much better. My knees were getting crampy sitting so long. It might mess up my hair more than I like, but this makes me like convertibles more." She looked at Ania's heels that were now hooked on the ugly sparkling lace and feather on the train. "Luke, let's take her to our hotel. Even if walking turns out to be the best course of action for her, which I don't think it will, she can't walk in those spikey designer heels and that tailored mermaid dress."

"Mermaid dress?" Luke asked looking at Ania.

"You're such a man's man. That is what you call a wedding dress that tapers to the knees and flairs out."

"Mais, I didn't know dat either," Tanté Izzy said, standing like Ruby. "Dis does feel good. My knees were gettin' crampy too."

Standing now, the energetic older woman looked tinier than she appeared sitting in the back seat of the sports car. And, how odd she was dressed. Ania had not noticed it before when her mind was focused on escaping the wedding and not getting killed. Did all little old Cajun ladies dress like this? Was it common for them to wear clothes like Tanté Izzy's bright pink pants under a gold shirt with rhinestone letters and a black leather fleur dis lis on the front of it? Maybe displaying the name of a favorite American football team on a shirt, the New Orleans Saints in her case, was a common Cajun practice. Maybe, wearing tennis shoes completely covered with large black and gold rhinestones and a wide-brim straw hat were too.

"I can see why it's called a Mermaid dress." Tanté Izzy nodded, switching her attention back to Ania's clothes. "It sure is a pretty dress."

Ania felt nervous laughter bubble in her throat. Pretty? This gown was awful and so over the top. Of course, so were Tanté Izzy's clothes. Not in the same way that her gown was. Her gown was more appropriate for a Las Vegas showgirl on stage than someone getting married. Dorek had picked out the gown and sent it over for her to wear that morning. He'd forgone a traditional wedding gown that would've been worn by the brides in her homeland, despite his bluster that he wanted a wedding that honored their traditions.

Luke folded his arms over his chest. "We can't sit in this parking garage all afternoon," he began, his voice deep and even. "It's a waste of time and time is not something I have to waste." He waved for her to get in the car and Ania felt like diving into the front seat head first. She preferred to drive out of the parking garage into the city streets over walking into them. Careful to not show her excitement for the offer because it might scare them away knowing how desperate she truly was, she moved slowly with fake calm toward the car.

"Ruby's right. You can't walk around town in that...dress and those shoes. I imagine your fiancé is combing the streets on the off chance that you are. I don't like you involving these nice ladies in your runaway bride adventure with men who don't have a problem firing their weapons at the car they're in. Hell, Miss Mitchell from Lithuania, I'm totally against you going to their hotel room and continuing to involve them in your problems. But, I also can't in good conscience abandon you in parking garage with danger lurking nearby."

He waved for her to get in the car again. Ania turned and sat in the front seat butt first. The veil yanked her head to the side as it got caught on the handle to the door. "Oh," she exclaimed, trying to pull it free. The rough fabric tugged against her bare arm and neck, making it feel like a brush burn beneath it. Luke jumped out of the car and came around to help her. He squatted next to her, his jeans tight against his long legs. She knew they would be as muscular as his arms. Yet, she was less frightened of him then she was earlier. He yanked hard on the veil. The sound of the fabric ripping had Ruby gasping.

"Don't you worry, Ruby," Ania said. "I shall never wear this thing again."

"Yes, but you could've sold it on eBay."

Ania's eye widened. "How much do you think I can get for it?"

"Well, I don't know. The dress must've cost a couple of thousand dollars or more so you should be able to get at least seven hundred dollars for it used."

"Oh my God. That much? How long does it take to sell on eBay? Is it hard to do?"

Luke blew out a breath. "So, I assume you don't have any money or access to it, either," he said, stuffing the train and bottom of her dress around her feet. "Of course, not. No purse or hidden money on you. No car stashed for a speedy escape. No family or friends to call. And, no police to help you from being shot at." Luke looked up at her and she felt the heat from his light eyes and the frustration in his frown. "Ania, what would you have done if we weren't in the parking lot when you ran away from your wedding? You had to have thought about that before you ran."

"Of course I thought about running away and the many things to be prepared to do it. But in thinking these things, I quickly learned that it is very much not possible. Oh, but then, like a miracle, it was." She shook her head and looked down at the feathers she twisted in her hands. "I knew I'd rather die trying to get away then have a wedding night with...him and have my heart and soul murdered."

"Mais, I've never know'd anyone so afraid of da one eyed snake to think about it like dat." Tanté Izzy said to Ruby. "She's a virgin bride."

Chapter Three

"I want to speak to Ania alone," Luke said to Tanté Izzy and Ruby as he sat on the small, dark green sofa in the tiny area designated as a living room in the all-suite hotel where the women were staying. Ania stood with her back to the door, looking like she was ready to make a quick exit at any moment. Tanté Izzy, who stood a head and shoulders shorter—and then some, stood between them. Both women were looking at him, Ania with hooded eyes filled with uncertainty and Tanté Izzy's direct with concern. He supposed he didn't blame them. He hadn't hidden his opinion that he didn't think Ruby and Tanté Izzy should get involved with this runaway bride who he all but called a liar when she gave them her crazy story about her name.

"She'z been through a rough day," Tanté Izzy said, her cloudy green eyes never wavering from him. "She needs to rest."

"It won't take long." Luke turned his palms to face up. "By the time you and Ruby find her something to wear in your suitcases, we'll be finished talking."

"Come on, Tanté Izzy," Ruby said from where she stood behind Luke near the kitchenette. "You know Luke. It'll be fine." Ruby smiled at Ania. "Talk to our Luke. He's a clever man. He can look at a muddy, uneven, weed infested piece of land and not only figure out how, but actually turn it into a beautiful homestead where a family can thrive. He can take the bad and make it good."

Ania looked at Luke as if she was trying to see the man that Ruby described. Doubt, apprehension and maybe a little curiosity was visible. Luke felt her indecision and worry too. It was as heavy as a thick, humid, Louisiana summer evening after it had rained. The swell of her round breasts rose and lowered over the bodice of her low-cut dress with each breath she took. Her shoulders were visibly stiff, her arms pressed tight against her sides—she looked like a woman who didn't have many options, or she would've certainly put herself out of her misery and walked out of the room.

"I think I've gotz a pretty shirt-dress that she can wear," Tanté Izzy said, walking toward the adjacent bedroom. Ruby followed her. "Youz know what one I'm talkin' about. The cotton dress with da magnolia pattern." They closed the bedroom door behind them.

"Please sit," Luke said, waving to one of the two wooden ladder-back chairs at the small dining table. "Would you like something to drink? A soda? Water?"

She walked to the table and sat. As she moved, the ever present sound of swooshing fabric followed her.

"No. Thank you."

He nodded.

"I know you are not pleased with me being here," she began, not waiting for him to speak first. "I will leave as soon as I change my clothes."

"Do you have a plan, Ania?" If that is who you are, he was about to say, but realized he really didn't care what her real name was. All he cared about was that she leave in a way that would satisfy Tanté Izzy and Ruby...and him.

"No plan. Just a goal." She looked away and again, there was the swooshing sound of fabric rubbing against fabric.

"Well that's a start, I guess."

"Yes. You must understand that you need a goal to start or you just turn in circles getting nowhere." She sighed and her shoulders seemed to relax a little. "Why do you see an ugly piece of land and build a family homestead on it? Was it for your wife and children?"

Luke smiled, her accent, Lithuania or whatever it was, seemed to roll off her tongue easily. If she was faking it, she was really good at doing so. The way she made all of the vowels sound look the "ee" sound made her a little hard to understand at times too. And the way she added an extra syllable with words with "r" in the middle, had him smiling. "Nah. It's for other people's families. I'm a builder. I have a construction company. I build houses and commercial buildings."

Her eyes widened as she nodded. "You are a carpenter. My grandfather was a carpenter."

"I'm not a carpenter." Hell, he hadn't actually driven a nail in a long, long time. His business had gotten too big, too demanding, for him to do that anymore. Sometimes he missed it though. He leaned back and folded his arms over his chest. "Once you change out of your wedding dress, where will you go? What do you plan to do?"

"I said I don't have a plan...yet."

"Okay. Then tell me what is your goal?"

She didn't answer right away and in the silence they heard Ruby and Tanté Izzy speaking Cajun French to one another. He had no idea what they were saying. He may have lived and worked in southern Louisiana for the last few years, but he'd only learned the slang phrases.

"Actually, I'm still working on the goal, too." She reached up and tried to take off the torn veil. He noticed she was doing so with more care than she'd used when she was balling the fabric in his jeep.

"You know you can't stay here. We're all leaving tomorrow. Ruby and Tanté Izzy have morning flights. I'm driving back to Louisiana. We can't help you." Her hands paused where she was pulling out hairpins from her very dark hair. "Do you have any money?"

She shook her head as she freed the veil and looked at it. "I will after I sell my wedding clothes on the eBay." She carefully folded it and placed it on the table. She looked around the room. "I need a computer."

"It could take a while to sell it and get the money." Crap. He knew what that meant. "I'll give you some money. Enough to get you where you need to go."

Her eyes widened and her hand flew to her neck. The shocked expression on her face told him that she might need more than a few hundred bucks. More than he had intended to give her. So be it. He'd give her what she needed.

"How much money do you need to get where you're going?"

"It is very complicated. Money is not my only problem."

He didn't want to know what her problem was. Yet, if he could do something to get her to leave faster, then he should. "Tell me what your problem is, Ania, and maybe I can help you figure out what to do." He stood, went to the refrigerator and got a bottle of water. He lifted it to her, in a silent offer, although he knew she'd just refused the offer a few minutes before. She shook her head no. Then she shook her head no again.

"You best not know."

"Fine. Honestly I don't really want to know. I just want you to go, and to not place Tanté Izzy and Ruby in danger in the middle of your problems. I also don't want you to think you can use them for financial gain." She folded her hands in her lap and looked down at them. She was a tall woman, but sitting there so slim, and hunched over, she seemed vulnerable and tiny.

Oh hell.

"What I am saying is, I don't want you to count on any of us for a solution to your problems. If you know that, then you can start looking elsewhere...sooner. It is in your best interest and ours if you do that."

"Yes, I know. I will take the bus," she said. "That will be good. No?"

"Yes."

She smiled a tight smile. "I have plan now."

"You have plan now," he repeated just as she had.

"Tanté Izzy and Ruby will be good with that too, no?"

"Yes." He nodded, but wasn't exactly sure that was true.

"I don't want to cause them any trouble. They are nice people." She swallowed hard and her eyes brightened with tears. "It's been a while since anyone was that nice to me." Her head popped up, like she had said more than she wanted too.

"I'm sorry things have been rough for you, Ania." He took a sip of his water. "So, we are in agreement. After you borrow that dress from Tanté Izzy and you say your thank yous and goodbyes, you are going to leave, right?" With a tidy sum to get her on the bus and to where she needed to go.

She ran her hand over the veil as she looked at it. "Yes. I go."

He reached into his back pocket and pulled out his wallet. "Six hundred should get you a decent hotel room tonight, a meal and a bus ticket. And for the next few nights." He put the money on the table.

She lifted her torn, dirty veil and handed it to him. "I give you my gown too. That should be square."

He smiled. "I don't want your wedding gown."

"I will not take your money. I cannot do such a thing and keep my pride. This is all I have to give you."

"Consider it a wedding gift."

She started to laugh. It was light and sweet and happy. Her eyes twinkled and her face seemed to glow. For the first time he realized just how beautiful she was. Oh, he'd noticed she had a sexy, killer body, long legs and narrow waist. He had even noticed that her small nose, wide mouth and high cheek bones formed a really pretty face. He just hadn't seen that spark that made a woman beautiful, until she laughed. Yeah, it was probably the thing her fiancé had noticed when he'd fallen for her. The thing he was willing to fight for to keep.

Yeah, fighting for her with his wits was one thing, but drawing a weapon and shooting at her was something else.

"Your fiancé..."

"He was never my fiancé," she interrupted.

"I'm sorry, but that doesn't compute, Ania. You were about to marry the guy."

Tanté Izzy took that moment to walk into the room carrying a light blue dress with large cream colored magnolias on it. Each button down the front was the size of a fifty-cent piece...and bright pink.

"Okay, youz had enough time talking. Now it'z time to get her dressed." Tanté Izzy handed the dress to Ania. "Dis is da dress I talked about earlier. Isn't it pretty?"

"Yes," she agreed, smiling.

"Ruby is in the bedroom waiting to help you out of dat wedding dress."

"Thank you very much." Ania stood, kicked the fabric away from her feet. She picked up the money on the table and handed it to Luke. She lowered her voice so only he could hear what she had to say. "I will not take money I did not work for or earn. Thank you for your kind gesture." She turned and walked to the bedroom.

"Youz satisfied now dat youz had your little talk wit her?" Tanté Izzy asked.

"Satisfying isn't what I'd call our conversation." He stood and walked to the kitchenette, grabbed a bag of BBQ chips from the counter and opened it.

"Did she tell you why she ran and why dat man tried to shoot her? Dat just ain't normal."

"No, it isn't." He stuffed a few chips in his mouth. "I didn't ask why she ran and she didn't volunteer the information."

"Dat would've been my first question." She stared at him for a few seconds. Luke felt disapproval in her gaze. "Dat girl is in big trouble that goes beyond leaving someone at da altar. I can feel it in my bones. And, I, for one, ain't goin' to abandon her when she needs a friend."

"Friend, yes. She should call a friend. We are strangers." He sat on the chair Ania had just vacated. It was still warm from her body heat. "We know nothing about her. We probably don't even know her real name. You do know she is probably lying to us about that and where she is from."

"Of course, she'z lyin'. Wouldn't you if you just ran away from a weddin' with a group of crazy men tryin' to hurt you? She's scared. The whole thing is embarrassin' and she doesn't know if she can trust us to not call him or someone who might bring him to her. For all she knows, we could've been in the parkin' lot because we were about to attend da weddin' as her fiancé's guests."

Luke hadn't considered that. "That's a good point, except that we weren't dressed like we were attending a wedding. We are all dressed like tourists. Me in jeans and you and Ruby in those 'Who Dat' shirts."

"Maybe she didn't notice in her panicked state." She pointed to his phone clipped to his belt. "Why don't you look in dat thing to see if youz can find her name in the weddin' announcement in da newspaper."

"Why? What difference would it make if we find her name in there?"

"Mais, it don't matter to me, none," Tanté Izzy frowned. "It'z just somethin' to do while we sit here. Besides, it's kind of like being on CIS or Law and Order. We'ze are just tryin' to solve a mystery." She waved her finger to his phone again. "Check and see."

Luke put the chip bag down, grabbed a paper napkin from the holder on the table and wiped his hands. He unclipped his phone and started an internet search of the Atlanta newspapers for wedding announcements of anyone with the name Ania.

"Wouldn't you prefer I spend the time rescheduling our Walking Dead Tour for tonight?"

"Do youz think Ania would like to come?"

Luke glanced up from his phone, hoping he'd see Tanté Izzy smiling as if she was just joking. She had picked up the veil and was examining it. There wasn't a hint of a smile on her face. She began brushing away at the smudges. She was dead serious. She had befriended Ania as easily as she had him when they met at the Christmas on the Bayou celebration. The big difference was he'd met her through mutual friends and he'd gotten to know her over time while he was working in her hometown of Cane. That really mattered little, he realized. Tanté Izzy now spoke of Ania as "we" not "her".

"Nothing is showing in the Atlanta-Journal Constitution for anyone named Ania. Nothing came up in that newspaper or in the over a dozen other Atlanta newspapers. None of the brides listed had any eastern European sounding names either."

"Did youz look for da last name Mitchell?"

Luke grunted. He didn't bother telling her that Mitchell was probably as much a lie as her name being Ania. The only way he might discover who she was, was by calling the Swan House at the Atlanta History Center and asking them.

"What time is da Walking Dead tour tonight?" Tanté Izzy asked as she still worked on the veil.

He went to the website for the tours. "Sorry. There's no way we can make it in time. The last tour is in an hour and Atlanta is an hour away from Senoia." He looked at Tanté Izzy. "I had no idea that Senoia was such a haven for movie and TV show locations. Did you know that *Fried Green Tomatoes, Pet Sematary II*, and *Drop Dead Diva* were all filmed in Senoia?"

"Mais, dat's a dumb question. Of course I did." She rolled her eyes. "Dat's why we wanted to go dere. That and because we'ze were hoping to see *Da Walking Dead* being filmed. I don't want to be in da TV show, though. I don't want to look like a zombie whose been buried for two weeks before I start walkin' around town." Her hands rested on the veil and she looked at Luke. "Did youz know I was in a movie filmed back in Cane? I had me a speaking part too."

"Imagine that. I'm friends with a real-life movie star."

"Dat you are." She nodded.

Twenty minutes later, Ania walked out of the bedroom with Ruby. Luke felt like the wind had been kicked out of his lungs. She was stunning. The heavy make-up had been washed off of her face and there was only a little bit of shine on her full lips. Her hair that had been pulled up under the veil, now hung, soft and loose in full waves down her back almost to her waist. She didn't wear any earrings or rings. She did have what looked like a pink ribbon wrapped three times around her tiny wrist with a single silver medal on it.

But, it was her eyes that drew him in most. They looked even bluer than they had earlier, seeming to match the powder blue color of the background of the dress she wore. The light, soft shade of the magnolias on the dress matched her creamy skin.

"Dat looks almost as good on you as it does on me," Tanté Izzy said, earning a huge smile from Ania. "I like da way you have da sleeves folded up to your elbows and I like da way it fits you a few inches above your knees. It fits me below my knees."

Luke thought the shorter length looked good on her too. She had nice, long, straight legs that he'd briefly glimpsed when she was trying to carry the heavy train of her wedding dress.

"We just need to get her some shoes," Ruby said, smiling and pointing to Ania's bare slender feet. "Our shoes didn't fit, so she'll just have those beautiful, but very tall stilettos until we do."

Luke frowned. There was that 'we' again when they spoke about Ania.

"Doesn't she look nice, Luke?" Ruby asked, a big smile on her face.

"Yes," he said, looking back down at his phone. "Much better than the wedding dress. She'll blend in now."

Ruby huffed. "Ania would never blend in anywhere. She is a real beauty. The kind that people write stories about. In fact, she reminds me of a young Elizabeth Taylor."

Tanté Izzy clapped her hands together. "I can see dat. Oh, I think maybe she looks more like Scarlet O'Hara from *Gone with the Wind*. We need to find you a pretty red dress like she wore in da movie."

Ania started laughing and the room seemed to brighten around her. "Oh-feedle-dee-dee," her thick accent made the familiar phrase sound quite different, but her joy made it charming and Tanté Izzy and Ruby started laughing with her. "You ladies are very generous with your words. I love Vivien Leigh. And, Scarlet O'Hara is a heroine for me."

This was a female-bonding, love-fest if ever Luke had seen one. Not good. He feared Ania would be moved in and living in Tanté Izzy's house in Cane by tomorrow afternoon. Just as he was ready to spoil their hen party by trying to resolve the problem at hand, Luke's phone started to ring, giving them a reprieve.

He looked down at the phone and knew he had to take the call from his long-time manager. He'd asked the man to run the numbers on the specific timbers that were listed for the park benches in the Magnolia Row community if they got the job. "Hold on," Luke said into the phone as soon as he answered, then turned to the women in the room. "I'm going to take this call in the hall. While I'm gone, y'all work out the when, how and what time Ania's going to the bus station."

"Bus station?" Ruby gasped.

"You're going to leave Atlanta by bus?"

"Yes," he heard Ania say as he opened the hotel room door. "It will be good. I can ride the bus for free. The bus company has a runaway safe ride program I read about. They give runaways a free ride. Four hundred runaways got rides last year. It is good, yes?"

"No!" Tanté Izzy and Ruby said at the same time.

"That is for runaway kids," Ruby all but shouted. "Not runaway brides."

Luke closed the door behind him.

Oh, hell. This was not going to be as easy as he hoped.

Chapter Four

Ania was back to having no plan only a goal.

She had hoped she could get a free bus ride out of town to somewhere safe and warm. A warm, safe city would've been good if she didn't find a place to sleep at night and had to live like the homeless. Ania had been in some very difficult and challenging situations in her life, but never had she been without a safe place to sleep at night. She rubbed the sides of her arms against the chill that raced through her body. A chill caused by a bone deep fear and desperation. Maybe she should have taken Luke's money and promised to pay him back.

No. That was a promise she wasn't sure she could keep. Ania Darska's always kept her promises and her word.

"Ania, do you have anyone you can call to help you?" Ruby sat on the sofa and motioned for Ania to sit with her.

"No," she answered honestly as she sat next to Ruby. "But, that is okay. I will find a way."

"I know youz will," Tanté Izzy said as she sat at the dining table. "But youz have to let us help you today when things are real difficult."

She rubbed her special medal at her wrist before resting her hands in her lap. "Can you help me sell my gown on eBay? That is all I need."

"I can, but it takes time," Ruby said, her tone confident and firm. "And, I think we have to get the dress laundered before we can take photos of it to put online. You'll never sell a dirty or torn wedding dress."

"Ruby and I have sewn all our lives. We can fix it up for you."

"Great idea, Tanté Izzy. We'll take her dress with us when we fly home tomorrow and get it looking like new. Then, I'll get Jewell, she's my cousin by marriage, to help me sell it for you. She can either put it in her Second Chance Consignment store or online or both."

"You know, Ruby, her dress isn't da only thing that can fly home with us." Tanté Izzy smiled.

Ruby clapped her hands. "Ania, you can come home with us."

Ania felt tears burn her eyes. These women were so kind and generous. She would love to go home with them, but she could not involve them in her troubles further. Her life was very much in danger. Just being with her would put them in danger too if Dorek found her with them.

Ania sucked in a breath and brushed away her tears. "I am very touched in my heart by your offer," she began. "Very much so. But, I cannot accept..."

"What choice do you have, Ania?" Ruby said, much in the tone her very own mother would have if she was alive.

"I have choices," she said, not liking any of them. "Besides, I do not have a passport or identification to fly."

"Can we go get it?" Tanté Izzy asked. "I don't mind a little B and E, me.

"B and E?" What was she talking about?

"Breaking and entering," Ruby explained. "It's a legal term."

"Legal? You mean illegal. Oh no. It would be too dangerous."

"Why would it be dangerous to go into your own place? What is going on with your fiancé Ania," Ruby asked, but before she was forced to lie again to these ladies, there was a knock on the hotel room door. Ania jumped up and rushed to look through the peephole. If it was Dorek, she would rush out the door and give herself up to him so he did not harm Ruby and Tanté Izzy.

"It's Luke," she said on an exhale as she opened the door. As soon as he walked in, his phone began to ring again.

"I've got to take this," he said and walked back out into the hall.

"He works all of the time," Ruby said, as Ania returned to sit next to her on the sofa. "We were lucky he made time to spend with us this afternoon." She looked at Ania. "You were lucky too. If he didn't have to go to the Swan House to take photos for work, we wouldn't have been there when you needed a get-away car."

A knock sounded on the door again. Ania rushed back as she had before and once again it was Luke.

"Busy night. There are a lot of fires I have to put out," he said, walking straight in to sit at the dining table near Tanté Izzy.

"Oh, are you a fireman too?" Ania asked.

Luke laughed. "Hardly."

Ruby smiled. "That's just a saying that means he's taking care of problems."

"You say the most confusing things in America," Ania shook her head. "Since coming to America three years ago, I have been studying idioms. This putting out fires is a new one. I can understand why it is said, but so many other ones just do not make sense, like *hitting the books, hit the sack, beat around the bush, ring my bell...*"

"How about *I've got an axe to grind* and *putting on the dog,*" Ruby said, laughing.

"I'ze got one," Tanté Izzy piped in from where she sat at the dining table. "*He's got da gumbo.*"

"I don't know what you all are talking about," Ania laughed. "What does *he got da gumbo* mean?"

"His pants are too big," Ruby answered, her face red and bright from laughing. She fanned her face. "That's a Cajun idiom, not American."

"I shall never learn them all," Ania said, meaning it. Especially since she would not be in America long enough to learn them. She would have no use for such things in Poland, or whatever country she found a safe home. She looked at Luke who was typing something on his phone. He was probably still putting out fires.

"Well the good news is your English is very good and you communicate so well, you'll do just fine," Ruby said, picking up a magazine and fanning her face with it.

"Are you well? You are very red?"

"It's just da her-mones," Tanté Izzy said. "It is her man-o-pause."

"I don't understand. Is that an idiom, too?"

"No, it's just my change of life."

Ania looked at her concerned. How was she changing her life? Ruby didn't seem to be very worried about changing it either? Maybe it was for a good purpose. Like her own change of life would be once she worked it out.

If she worked it out.

"It seems many of us have the change of life," she told them. "This is good, no?"

"Mais, youz are way too young for a change of life," Tanté Izzy said, folding her arms over her chest. "How old are you?"

"Twenty-seven."

"Y'all are not on the same page," Luke said, "and that is an idiom, too."

Ania smiled. So, he was listening even as he was using his phone.

Ruby got up and walked to Tanté Izzy, saying something to her in Cajun French. Luke watched them, but didn't say anything. His expression did speak volumes though. Ania could see he either didn't like what they were saying or that they were saying it so he couldn't understand them. After a few moments of speaking back and forth, Tanté Izzy looked at Luke and spoke to him directly.

"We'ze a decision."

He clipped his phone to his belt. "I can tell I am not going to like it."

"Go, on," Ruby told Tanté Izzy with a nod. "Don't let him intimidate you with that surly act."

"Mais, he cain't intimidate me," Tanté Izzy said, narrowing her eyes at Luke. "Youz have to be uncertain to be intimidated. I'm never uncertain."

"Tell me what decision the two of you made," Luke said, knowing he wasn't going to like it before hearing it.

She took a step closer to Luke. "We'ze decided that youz need to be well fed to hear what we have to say. A man hears what a woman has to say better when his belly is full. We're are orderin' man's food from da steak house next to da hotel and eatin' it here. How do you like youz steak cooked."

Luke looked at her a moment, his eyes steady on hers. "Medium rare."

His phone dinged that he'd received another message. He kept his eyes on Tanté Izzy a moment longer before retrieving his phone and looking down at it.

Chapter Five

Apparently a really good steak and potato dinner finished off with warm peach cobbler could make a man not only hear what two crazy women had to say, but agree to it. A great meal and the fact that it sounded logical at the time. He didn't like it, nor did he want to do it, but until he could figure out an alternate plan, he'd agree to it.

"I am sorry for this inconvenience," Ania told him for the fourth time since dropping Tanté Izzy and Ruby off at Hartsfield airport. She'd also said it a fifth time when they left the Catholic church where he had taken them to Sunday mass before heading to the airport. By the frown on her pretty coral lips, she didn't seem to like the situation any better than he did. He found some satisfaction in that.

Some.

"Look, Ania, we're stuck together for the next week," he said, not trying to soften his tone or words. "You're riding with me on a long, scenic route from Atlanta to Cane, but it's important and necessary. I'll be stopping along the way to take photos of gardens, buildings, homes and architectural features for a project I'm working on. I get that you're in a jam. A jam that was totally you're doing when you raced out of your wedding with no money, no passport and no idea where you were going. Now, I'm in a jam too. It's done. Let's not talk about it anymore."

She slipped off her four inch studded shoes and sat back in her seat. Her eyes however, gave away her anxiety as she constantly looked around them.

"What kind of car does your fiancé drive?"

"He was never my fiancé." She shook her head. "A black Escalade with big tires. Most of his...friends drive that kind, too, or they drive what I heard them call, muscle cars." She looked at him. "What is a muscle car? Is that an idiom?"

"Nah. A muscle car is a car with a lot of power, or muscle. It's an American made sports car with a big engine. Most muscle cars were built in the 1960's and 70's, but some are later models than that."

"I look for that, too."

"How long do you think he'll be out looking for you? Maybe, he's realized it was stupid to go after someone who clearly doesn't want him."

"He'll never give up."

"Never? Is he some sort of mentally unstable person or is there another reason that I should know that he'll keep looking for you?'

"He is like spoiled brat," she said on a sigh. "He wants what he wants."

Before Luke gave that any consideration, his phone rang. It was Trent, the assistant to the CEO of Magnolia Row. "I'm going to take a call over the car's speaker," he told Ania. "Do not repeat anything you hear of my conversation." She nodded. "Good morning, Trent."

"Morning, Luke. I've got a new set of plans for the clubhouse. I'd like you to look at it and send us your feedback by tomorrow morning. We want to know if you think the changes will affect our budget, and we want to know if you see any problems with the designs. We want to make all of the changes before we award a construction company with the job. You know, we want a 'No Change Order' project."

"Yes, I know. I'll take a look at it and get back to you." Luke put on his blinker and merged north onto the interstate. "Should I expect any more changes in the proposed designs or is the final one?"

"Of course you should. You know we'll be tweaking it until we sign contracts with the construction company that gets this project."

"I look forward to seeing them." They ended the call after a brief good-bye.

"Where are we going?" Ania asked, stress clear in her voice and by the way she fidgeted with her bracelet. "We are going north, back into Atlanta instead of west toward Louisiana?"

"Like I said before, we're taking the long route because of my work. It's why it's going to take a week instead of twelve hours to get there," Luke answered, but he was thinking about having to find a hotel with good internet service and a good printer by three or four if he was going to have enough time to go over the designs, send his assessment to his team, and then write up a report on it to submit to Trent in the morning.

"Where is it that we are going?" she asked again, her voice sounding shaky.

He looked at her. "The Atlanta Botanical Gardens. Is that a problem?"

She didn't answer, but she started to bite her bottom lip. When he took the midtown exit to the botanical gardens, she slid lower in her seat.

"Ania, are we in a part of town that we are more likely to run into your spoiled brat guy?"

She nodded. "This is where he lives and works."

"Do you know your way around here well enough to get me to the botanical gardens without passing right in front of his house or work?"

"No. I only know how to catch the MARTA to get to the library and the Margaret Mitchell house."

"The Margaret Mitchell house, huh? Is she a relative of yours?"

She looked down at her hands a moment and shook her head no. "Can you go to the gardens from another way other than Midtown?"

He zoomed out on the map on the navigation screen on the dash. "Yeah. I haven't lived in Atlanta for a long time, but I can get us there another way. But, Ania, we're technically already in Midtown." He glanced at her as she slid even lower in her seat. "This is insane. We should call the police if you're that afraid of him."

"No. We cannot. You have to trust me that I know why we cannot, Luke."

"I'm not like Tanté Izzy and Ruby. I don't trust blindly. Give me something so I believe you."

She didn't answer, but she looked at him.

"The truth, Ania. If we're going to make this road trip work, I need you to trust me too."

Her shoulders dropped and she nodded. "He has many friends that are police. I do not know who to trust with my safety. And, Luke, he will call his friends to make sure he gets me." She sucked in a shaky breath. "He is very motivated since I did not marry him and fulfill his plans. I humiliated him in front of his friends and colleagues. He will want to punish me to prove that no one can get away with doing that to him. He will not stop until he does."

Luke's stomach tightened and his temper flared. He felt like fighting this man. Right here. Right now. This son-of-a-bitch had vowed to love and take care of Ania when they decided to marry. No matter how humiliated her fiancé felt being jilted, Luke didn't understand how the man went from loving her enough to marry her to wanting to physically hurt her. Just like he didn't understand how a man loved, married a woman, had a child with her and then, when they awaited the happy event of their second child, decided he didn't want a life with her and their children.

No, her fiancé wasn't Luke's father, but the jerk was cut from the same warped, tainted cloth. If the selfish bastard showed up, Luke would defend Ania against him.

"Does this guy have a name? I can't keep calling him your fiancé"

"He was never my fiancé."

"Yeah, I got that, but I need something to call him when we're talking about him. And, Ania, don't tell me his name is Rhett Butler."

She smiled. "I would not do that. I like Rhett too much." She turned to look up at him. "His name is Dorek."

"No last name, huh?" He shrugged. "Fine. It doesn't really matter."

A few minutes later, Luke passed the entrance to the botanical gardens and turned on to its narrow service road. Here, if he didn't get kicked out first, he could park his car out of sight if Dorek or his friends showed up. That seemed like a long shot since no one had followed them. Still, since they were in his Midtown neighborhood it was possible that he'd drive by the botanical gardens parking lot and spot his car. He hadn't discussed it with Ania, but his BMW was easily recognizable not only because of its special deep red color, but because it had been decked out with custom rims. The top was up on his convertible now, but if Dorek or his buddies had any car sense, that wouldn't throw them off.

"We can walk from here," he said after parking next to the dumpsters he was certain wouldn't be emptied on a Sunday. Ania started to slip on her crystal studded wedding shoes. "Wait," he reached behind him into his backpack, "use my flip-flops until we can get you something better to walk in."

"I look like I am walking on log boats," she laughed, looking at the black rubber flip flops that were much too big for her slender feet.

"We'll go to the gift shop and see if they sell any shoes there." He reached into his backpack again, pulled out a Marcelle Family Construction baseball cap and placed it on her head. "Not much of a disguise, but it'll do."

Ania twisted her hair and shoved it under the hat. "Better?"

Luke paused from taking his camera out of its bag and looked at her. The long column of her neck was exposed, its pale, flawless skin mustn't have been touched by the sun in a very long time. Her neck looked delicate, vulnerable and damn sexy. "Yeah." He managed, turning to open the door. He was going to buy her a scarf too.

They walked to the botanical gardens entrance, got their tickets for the thirty-acre gardens. It was fairly crowded, but not overly so since it was still early in the day and the gardens had just opened. Ania remained vigilant, looking around for any signs of trouble, and even turning her back to a uniformed park guard as they passed through the entrance gates.

The tension he felt in her tight posture, seemed to dissolve as the sound of the swooshing water cascading through the fountains mixed with happily chirping birds. It transported them into another place that was peaceful and uncomplicated. A place where the strong scents of healthy soil and sweet blooming flowers filled their lungs. A place where cream colored butterflies with scalloped black edges, danced on tops of the orange, yellow and purple flowers. A place that could make a person feel as though they were in another time and place, and nothing bad could happen here. Ania stopped walking, turned in a slow circle with her mouth open in awe.

"I see what the sign means," she said, her voice barely above a whisper. "Atlanta Blooms. Look at all this color. It is magical," she whispered. "I had no idea it was here in Atlanta where I live." She pointed to the cheerful pink tulips filling a large boxwood lined flowerbed. "We have those in my homeland. What do you call them?"

"Tulips. The purple ones are pansies. Don't ask me the names of those tall fluffy deep blue ones that look like starfish."

"*Hiacynt*," she said in her native language. "We have them too." Her eyes seemed to be unfocused like a person who was daydreaming.

What are you thinking about Ania? Are you thinking of being back in your country during the springtime? Does it make you homesick? Luke thought about the times he felt homesick. It wasn't because he longed for the flowers or the house he thought represented home. It had been for the people who'd planted the flowers and occupied the space in his life. He shook off the feeling. That time was gone. They were gone. Looking back did no good.

He took her hand and led her on the path that meandered toward the visitor center and gift shop. Her delicate fingers felt warm and thin in his hand. He let go of her. Holding hands felt too intimate a thing to do with a stranger who shouldn't be in his busy life right now.

"After we get you some shoes that fit," he said to her, "I want to see the rock garden. If I get the contract I'm bidding on to build a gated neighborhood near New Orleans, I'd like to add a rock garden along the planned walking trails. Kids love to climb on rocks. I want to figure out how to make it look like God and Mother Nature put it there, not my workers. Rock gardens don't occur in nature in the deep south, but I discovered the horticulturist here made it look like it did by using native plants along with the big boulders they brought in."

"You are building a town?"

"For a client," he said as they walked on the well-groomed shell path. "And, it isn't a town. It's a community."

"That is special, to take all of the best that makes communities and villages good and to place it in a new place."

In the gift shop, they found pink and white rubber garden shoes that fit Ania and didn't look too terrible because of the huge, eccentric pink buttons Tanté Izzy had sewn down the front of the dress. As they made their way to the rock garden, Luke took photos of interesting sculptures and the way it was tucked harmoniously into a beautiful space that always had a bench, stool or rock to sit and contemplate or appreciate what was there. That was something he would add to the project. Places to stop and reflect. This community should have some private, quiet places to enjoy, not only public ones to share. He even took photos of beautiful, complicated Ania as she sat on a gray weathered oak swing and floated it over a sea of fragrant blue, white and yellow crocuses. She looked like a living sculpture in the gardens.

He would think of Magnolia Row and the people who lived there this way as he constructed each building, garden and space there. The idea of doing this made his heart race and head spin with excitement. It felt good, thrilling, challenging and fun—just as it had when he built his first house...but even better on this large-scale build.

Luke watched Ania as she got off the swing and started to walk toward him. It was nice seeing her enjoying the gardens. It was nicer that having her there reminded him of the fun reasons he wanted the Magnolia Row job. But, he didn't have time to think about all the nice things about Ania. His company couldn't afford him having flights of fancy thoughts. Not right now. Ania was a distraction. He had to be laser focused to win the Magnolia Row contract. Once he got the contract, then he would be able to do the kind of work he always wanted and to allow Marcelle Family Construction to grow.

A lot was riding on him doing it right. Just this morning, his accountant had reminded him how badly his company needed to win the contract. Not that he needed a reminder. He'd purposely risked everything to move into a more profitable segment of the construction industry. His employees were counting on him to close the deal.

"Luke, can we visit to the edible garden before we go to the rock garden," Ania asked when she reached him. "I heard that man tell his wife that there was a cooking demonstration in the outdoor kitchen with Chef Don Walker. He is very good. He has three different theme restaurants in Atlanta. He is very important."

"Sure. I want to get photographs of the vertical vegetable wall there. Let's go."

Ania took off ahead of him but as she reached the round raised garden filled with tomatoes, bell peppers, eggplant and other vegetable plants, she stopped, turned around and started running back from the way they'd come.

***

Ania saw Josef in front of the vertical wall of herbs and small vegetable plants at the same time he spotted her. Blood suddenly roared in her ears. The man known for the quickest temper of all of Dorek's men, lifted a phone to his ear as he took a step toward her.

"*Nie!*" Ania took off running. She heard his rapid footsteps on the gravel path behind her as she raced passed Luke, who gave her a startled look. She had no time for explanations. Heart pounding, she stumbled from the rubber garden shoes that were a little too wide for her feet. Thank God, she wasn't wearing Luke's giant flip-flops.

She raced out of the edible garden on to the main path, waving to people heading toward her to move out of the way. Her feet began to ache. The stiff shoes were meant to keep her feet dry in a wet garden, not run full-out on a hard path, but she didn't let it slow her down.

She couldn't.

Josef would catch her and take her to Dorek. Dorek. *Oh God. Is he here in the botanical gardens too?* Was she searching for her in another area of the garden? Were there others here to try to capture her? Was it Dorek who Josef called to say he found her? How did they know she was there?

Questions whipped around in her head like it was caught in a whirlwind with dust and debris. Her mind was not clear for anything except trying to escape. *Run. Run fast.*

If Dorek was here, he'd be headed her way—probably on the main path. Ania looked at the woodlands off to her left side. Without thinking where it would lead, she leaped over the boxwood hedges lining the path and ran into the canopy of maple trees.

"Ania," she heard someone shout her name. An American by the way he pronounced it. Luke. She looked over her shoulder without slowing down, past where Josef was leaping over the boxwoods. Luke was running too.

"Nie!" she called to him as he leaped over boxwoods and started to rush at an angle toward the trees. *Go away.* From the angle he was running he would reach her before Josef. "Don't slow down," Luke shouted to her. "Keep running."

"Go away, Luke," she tried to call to him, but the words just mingled with the heavy breathing from her fear and exertion. Oh, God. Dorek will know now that she had help. He'd know Luke was involved. She felt like throwing up.

Josef called to her from behind, telling her in Polish that she was making it worse by fleeing. His voice seemed to bounce off the bark of the trees and send a hard jolt of fear against her spine. Oh, God. How could it be worse? Dorek was going to kill her.

She heard Luke's heavy steps pounding just behind her, as he grabbed her hand and jerked her to the left and pulled her in another direction.

"Leave me alone," she shouted and tried to pull her hand free.

"Are you crazy?" He pulled her off again in another direction and after stumbling on a root, she righted herself and continued with him. "Shut up. Pay attention."

Ania had no time or breath to argue. He gave her no choice but to follow him. The ground began to slope and they had to grab hold of low hanging tree branches to help with the climb up the side of a hill, as voices seemed to get louder ahead of them. Who was there? Where was Luke leading her? The trees started to thin as a wide path opened before them. She looked behind them, she couldn't see Josef but she heard the sound of feet crunching over the fallen foliage.

He wasn't far behind.

"Here," Luke said, motioning toward a serpentine paved path. They ran along it and moved faster and easier than they had in the uneven underscore of the woodlands, although they were still surrounded by trees. The voices started to grow louder, but there weren't any people on the path. Then, Ania saw where the voices were coming from...above them on a concrete and steel structure meandering overhead ahead of them to get a birds-eye view of the woods. It was the Canopy Walk that she had seen on the posted map she had examined near the visitor's center.

They continued to run along the path, until they were under the heavy structure that was there to give visitors a birds-eye view of the woodlands.

"Ania."

The voice echoed through the oaks, hickories and poplar trees from above. It was Dorek. She recognized his voice, his tone and his correct pronunciation of her name. She looked up above her. He was flanked by two of his men. Dorek waved to her and smiled. Ania's blood turned to ice and slowed her stride. Luke took her hand into his again and tugged on her.

"Don't stop. The other guy is catching up." She turned and saw Josef on the path, racing toward them, his gun visible as his hoodie lifted over the waistband of his jeans.

On legs that felt like thick logs, she moved forward as Dorek shouted to her in Polish.

"You can't hide from me, my bride. I will have you." She heard the men next to him laugh.

Ania rushed ahead of Luke. *No. No. No.* The laughter echoing in her head.

"This way," Luke said, grabbing her hand and tugging her off the path, through the dense woods until they reached an open lawn. Ania tripped as the surface went from pine needles and dead leaves to groomed lawn. She fell to her knees cushioned by the grass. Luke picked her up under her arms, looked directly in her eyes. "You okay?"

"Yes."

"Then let's go. The others are here." Ania looked off to her right toward the beautiful tiered fountain beside a colorful garden filled with roses of different shades of pink, white, yellow and blue.

"Dorek is here."

"Which one is Dorek?" Luke asked as they started off across the lawn.

"Black jacket. Light hair."

"Big guy." He turned into another rose garden bordering the lawn. The freshly watered pink tipped yellow tea roses surrounded them in a rich, sweet, peaceful fragrance contradicting the horror of them running for their lives.

On the other side of the garden, were two small brick structures. Luke went to the first one, stopped and let go of Ania's hand. "Let me know if they're close," he told her, breathing hard. He reached into his pocket and pulled out a pocket knife. Ania didn't see how he did it, but he managed to pry the lock on the door open, he pulled her inside the small building that smelled like diesel and mechanical fluids and closed the door behind them, leaving them in complete darkness.

"Wh..." he put his hand over her mouth and she felt his breath on her ear.

"Shh." She nodded and he removed his hand.

She heard Dorek talking to his men from outside the building in Polish, telling them to split up and meet at the front gate in ten minutes. A voice that she thought must've been Josef's confirmed the time. Then, there was some cursing and boasting about who was the best tracker and would be the one to get Ania and the man with her. Dorek shouted to them to just capture her and to get rid of the man so he didn't bother them again.

Ania grabbed her stomach. She wanted to throw up.

Luke put his arm over her shoulder and pulled her against him. How did he know in the darkness that she was ill? Could he have known what they said before going off to search for her? Then she heard it. The handle on the door being rattled to try to open it.

Luke pulled her tighter against his side and she felt his breath on her ear again, warm and steady. "Don't move."

She nodded. Perspiration rolled in a long, slow path down the side of her face, down her chin, along her neck and between her breasts.

The person on the other side hit the door, probably trying to knock it open. She stepped in front of Luke. He wrapped his arms around her waist and pulled her fully against him. They were not breathing in unison. As his chest rose and fell in a steady pace against her back, her breathing was faster, almost as if she was sprinting. "It's okay. We've got this. No one will get you. I won't let him."

The door flew open and blinding light poured into the small building. Luke shoved Ania to the floor, picked up something that sounded like it contained liquid and threw it at the person now rushing into the room. Ania turned in time to see the man falling to the floor and the large metal container that had landed on him, roll to the floor with a loud bang. Luke grabbed her hand, jerked her to her feet and pulled her toward the door. The smell of diesel, unmistakable and heavy, filled the room.

As she moved past the man on the floor, she saw it was Dorek. Oh God, he had stayed behind to search the building as he sent his men off to look for her. If he captured Luke, he would kill him. He would kill her too. Her knees began to wobble. Her hands began to shake. She started to run. He grabbed her ankle and she screamed. "Nie!" She stumbled but managed to kicked out to free herself from his hold but her shoe had fallen off. Luke was suddenly there, kicking him in the ribs, over and over again. She looked around for something to use as a weapon, but Luke beat her to it. He picked up shovel and hit Dorek over the head with it. He went still.

"You okay?" Luke asked, grabbing her hand. She nodded. "Let's get the hell out of here before he comes to." Luke released her hand, took a roll of electrical tape from a hook where it was hanging and tied Dorek's hands and feet with it. "Time to go."

As Luke turned to leave, Ania bent over, took Dorek's gun from his waistband where the sunlight streaming in through the door shone like a lighthouse beacon onto the gun's chrome slide across the top. It sickened her to think that this might be the gun that she'd seen Dorek fire into the head of another human being. No. He wouldn't have kept it, she reasoned as she picked up her shoe and ran out of the building behind Luke. Coming out of the dark interior into the bright sunlight felt like shards of glass had been tossed in her eyes. She lifted her hand to shield them.

"Are you crazy?" Luke took the heavy gun she held against her forehead in the hand blocking the sun. "I'll hold the Glock." He made sure the safety was on, then stuffed the gun into the waistband of his jeans at the small of his back. He untucked his dark brown button down shirt and covered it. "Let's go."

"I am used to holding dangerous implements," she said, angry that he didn't trust her with the gun. The implements she was talking about might not be guns, but she had to be careful using them nonetheless. Her chef's knives were very sharp and had sliced her fingers on more than one occasion. Oh, she would take the gun back from Luke. It was hers. She had stolen it from Dorek, not him. Knowing that gave her a sense of power. Knowing she could protect herself using Dorek's gun gave her a sense of satisfaction. "I want my gun back."

Luke didn't answer her and she was forced to save the argument for later. She followed him behind the buildings to a gate that was posted with a sign that read Atlanta Botanical Gardens Employees Only when she heard Dorek's phone begin to ring from inside the maintenance building.

"They will come to look for him if he doesn't answer," Ania said as Luke jumped over the chain-link fence on the right side of the passcode locked gate.

"Then get the lead out."

"Do not talk in idioms when I am trying to think in English and my mind is jumbled with worry," she said, her tone sharp. Ania tossed her shoe over the fence and climbed over. Luke moved to help her down and she accepted his help, making sure to hold on tightly so he knew she was counting on his strength. His back muscles bunched beneath her hands as her hands slid to his hips. "Thank you," she said, looking up at him.

Then, she walked away, hiding that she'd just taken Dorek's gun from Luke. She held the gun in front of her as he walked ahead of Luke to the car.

Chapter Six

Luke drove in the direction of his next planned stop; east of Atlanta. Both he and Ania kept watchful eyes for suspicious cars behind them and those entering the interstate at each on ramp. As each mile added between them and the botanical gardens, Luke grew confident that they had given Dorek and his men the slip...this time.

"Ania, we can't keep doing this, you know?"

She exhaled a heavy breath and shifted in her seat. "If this has gotten too...what is the word I am looking for..."

"Dangerous?"

"No. Too frightening."

"Hell, yeah it is frightening," Luke admitted running his hand through his hair. "Ania, this is too dangerous for you to fight. It falls in the category of trained professionals fighting this battle. We were lucky back there. Hell, we were lucky to get away from your wedding yesterday. If it happens again, and I hope it doesn't, we may not be so lucky again."

"Maybe not. I think it is time I go." She looked out the window at the black SUV they were passing. Luke had already seen it and discounted it as being Dorek's when he saw the two children in car seats in the back. "I can survive this on my own. We will go our separate paths at your next stop. I think this is good. It is time. You helped me when I was most in trouble. I appreciate that very much."

"Survive on your own? With what resources?" he said, frustration making his words sound harsh and loud. His phone rang and he picked it up without looking to see who was calling. It was the vendor for the marine treated wood pilings he'd ordered for the wharf at the house they were finishing up in Cane. The vendor had a question about the order. Luke pulled off on the nearby exit and reached in the back seat for his iPad. As he pulled it out of his duffle bag, other folders fell to the floor and papers started to blow around in the back. Ania unbuckled her seat belt and made fast work of capturing the loose papers. Luke gave her a thumbs up.

"Ania you aren't taking off on your own," he said as soon as he hung up the phone. "Tanté Izzy and Ruby would have my head." They'd made that clear when they called to check on Ania after landing at the airport in New Orleans. "Ruby's exact words were *'You had better be taking care of that pau'vre bete' as if she was the princess of Lithuania and the annihilation of the free world depends on her being safe and sound.'*"

Ania smiled. "I also remember Tanté Izzy saying she would get the *traiteur* to put a zombie-*rougarou* curse on you if you did not keep me. Whatever a *traiteur* and a *rougarou* are, it sounds bad. I am guessing the one to issue the curse is a witch." She shrugged. "I write a note for you to give them. It will say I take responsibility for my safety because I want to."

"A note? Forget it. That won't satisfy them." He knew he was clenching his jaws because his teeth were starting to hurt. "We need to figure this thing out because being shot at and chased by spoiled brat thugs, is very serious."

"I told you it was serious from the beginning. I told you Dorek would never give up trying to get me back...or making sure I was dead." She handed him the file folders with the neatly stack of the papers on top of it. "This sudden understanding of this is not on my side. It is yours. I have lived with this knowledge for a very long time. At the wedding I took my chance to get away from it."

"You're right. I didn't fully understand how...bad this was." He put the folders and papers in his duffle bag and zippered it, then turned to face Ania. "Honestly, I didn't want to know. Now, I should know." Luke thought about that a minute, trying to separate what he needed to know from what he wanted to know. "Will Dorek keep searching for you?"

"Yes. He will not give up. I am too important to him. He wants to possess me. The most bad part is—I threaten him."

Oh, hell. He had to ask. He had to know how she threatened him. Damn. It was at the heart of why the man was willing to shoot at her and him in public places. Crap. Sure, maybe it was selfish of him to not want to know about her problems because it would interfere in his difficult work goals. He considered more self-preserving. Yet, he'd be a fool not to know the score since she brought it up. Every muscle in his body stiffened. Once she answered, he knew intuitively that his life would go from eight on the complications scale to ten-plus.

"How do you threaten a bad-ass like Dorek?"

She inhaled deeply. She looked away and he wondered if she would tell him the truth and if she didn't why wouldn't she? "He has very much pride. If I get away from him, he looks bad with his friends and business associates. It proves to them if he can not take care of big problem...um, me doing what he wants, then he can not do good work for them."

What she said rang true, but it also felt like she was not telling him everything. "I've worked with and witnessed controlling men like that," he admitted, trying to sort out what she said. "I've seen them lose their temper and focus to make stupid decisions. I've never seen anyone try to kill another person over it, although I've seen plenty of detective shows where that happened." He shook his head. "So, that's it. You threaten him because he is a control freak?"

She nodded. Her eyes still not meeting his.

"Okay. I still think we need to call the police. He's committed a few dozen crimes."

"Yes, he has," she said easily. "But, I beg for no police now. We are away from him. He is no place near. See?" She waved her hand in an arc around them.

He shook his head. He wouldn't call the police now, but he would if Dorek showed up again. Luke leaned over, reached under his seat, and pulled out the 9mm Ruger semi-automatic he had holstered there. She sucked in a breath and moved against her door. She slid her hand under her seat.

"Leave it. You don't need it," he said, knowing that she'd placed Dorek's gun under her seat when they'd gotten back to the car at the botanical gardens. "I'm not going to hurt you. I'm just showing you that I have a weapon in the car. I'm prepared to fight the spoiled brat to protect you and myself." Ania placed her hands in her lap. "I have a concealed carry permit and I know how to use this." He put his weapon back under the seat. "I get why you took the gun in the maintenance building. It kept Dorek from using it on us. I'm sure he's gotten another one by now. We should get rid of this one. Neither one of us has a permit for it and it will only mean problems if we get caught with it. We have enough problems. Plenty. This is one that we don't need to have."

Ania reached under the seat and tossed the pilfered Glock out of the open window.

"What the hell are you doing?"

"Getting rid of problem," she shouted, looking at him like he had gone mad. He didn't doubt he was looking at her the same way.

"What happens if a child finds it?" He opened his door and got out of the car.

"Why would a child walk here by the highway exit in the weeds?" She shook her head and opened her door. They both walked into the sweet smelling, tall grass beyond the shoulder. The red, clay ground was wet and squishy from the recent rain.

"Parents pull over to the side of the road all of the time to let their children pee."

"There is a lot of land and grass on the side of the road. It is very improbable that they will choose the very spot where the gun is located." She let out a loud sigh, leaning over to search through the stiff knee-high grass.

Luke slapped at his arm where a very hungry mosquito landed. "Ania, you just don't toss a dangerous weapon out of a car." He kicked aside the grass with his foot as he walked further from the car.

She slapped at something on her leg. "Where do you toss it?"

"Hell if I know," he mumbled.

"I'm sorry. I did not think it through." She moved in a straight line from the car, down a gentle slope toward the drainage ditch. "It was spontaneous. I never considered the *siku* stop to relieve the child."

She and Luke continued to search for fifteen minutes when Ania shouted, "I find it." She picked up the weapon by the grip with her finger and thumb. "It landed in the puddle."

Luke walked over and took the wet, dirty weapon from her. "Come on." He moved to the back of his car and opened the trunk where he kept a lint-free, towel that he used to clean his car. He handed it to Ania. "Clean your hands on this before I wrap the gun in it." As she wiped the wet, red Georgia dirt off of her hand, he turned his back to the road in case a car passed by. He removed the loaded magazine and tucked it into a compartment near the wheel well. After Ania handed him the towel he wrapped the Glock with it, not bothering to clean it, and put it into the toolbox he kept in his trunk. He'd dismantle it later and toss the parts away in the trash in several locations.

After cleaning their shoes, they climbed back into the car.

"I need you to tell me, truthfully," Luke said, turning Ania's face so she looked directly at him. The smooth porcelain skin felt cool and feminine under his work roughened fingers. He pushed aside the jolting realization of how good it felt to touch her and to think of her in a way other than as the woman who could make him lose his company. "Ania, I need to know. If I shoot Dorek or any one of his goons while I'm trying to protect us, will I be shooting the bad guys? Or will I be shooting a stupid, love-sick jerk and his misguided friends?"

She swallowed hard, and cleared her throat. "They are very, very bad men. They will not pause in shooting you or me or anyone who gets in their way. And, Luke they are all very good at getting people out of their way."

Luke nodded as he traced the outline of her jaw with his fingertips. "Okay. I know where I stand."

"You are sitting," she said, her voice a little breathier than it had been before. "I do not understand what you mean?"

"It's another idiom, Ania." Dropping his hand, he started the vehicle, and drove back onto the ramp toward the interstate. "It means I'm going to do what I must to keep us safe."

"Me too."

The adrenaline rush from their fight and flight, and probably the reassurance that Luke would protect her, allowed Ania to give into the tug to close her eyes once she was certain no one was following them. Then, with a big yawn she shifted to her side, tucked the edges of the dress beneath her thighs so it wouldn't continue fluttering in the wind from the top being down, and went to sleep. It bothered him that even after she'd been sleeping for an hour and forty minutes, her brows were scrunched into a frown. He imagined she hadn't really had a restful sleep in a long time.

Luke glanced at his reflection in the rearview mirror and saw that he was frowning too. It didn't surprise him. He was between a rock and a hard place–idiom use totally intentional. Ania was in real danger. If he'd any doubts about that before their visit to the botanical gardens, he didn't any longer. It was why he told her he would help protect her. Yet, he also realized that his demanding work schedule might not make him the person best suited for the job. Hiring a bodyguard might be his best course of action.

Getting a restraining order against Dorek seemed like a good move too.

Ania wouldn't like either of those options. She wouldn't accept Luke paying for a bodyguard that she couldn't afford. She would also continue to resist involving the police, which was necessary to acquire a restraining order.

He should call Jen.

His younger sister would know how to handle this situation since this was the kind of thing she dealt with as an assistant district attorney at the Fulton County District Attorney's office in Atlanta. He would've preferred meeting with Jen in person to discuss this, but she was in Chicago attending a National Prosecutors conference. He'd have to call her. He'd wait until tonight when he was alone and could speak to his sister freely.

Luke's phone rang and he quickly picked it up and took it off of the car speaker. He didn't want to wake Ania. The call was about the proposed east entrance gate for Magnolia Row. He had to review the designs and sourced material for the guardhouse interior as well as the placement of the guard's parking spot. When he finished the call, as was his habit when he was driving, Luke dictated the notes of what was discussed into his phone's memo-pad. He'd organize and place those notes into a file in his computer so he'd have it available if he couldn't recall a detail that was discussed. His attention to detail was what made him good at what he did.

Two work calls, a text and twenty minutes later, Luke pulled into the parking lot across from the Fitzpatrick Hotel where they were going to spend the night. He touched Ania's arm. "Wake up. We're here."

She immediately sat up and looked around. "Is everything okay?"

"Yeah, everything is fine." He waited for her to recompose herself; wipe her eyes, tuck her hair behind her ears, and straighten her dress that had twisted around her thighs as she slept. "We're at the hotel in Washington. We'll check in, then I need to get photos of a few things nearby."

"Washington? The capital of the United States? How long did I sleep?" She looked toward the tan brick Romanesque courthouse and its tall gothic clock tower across from the hotel. "This looks very different than what I've seen on TV."

Luke smiled. "This is Washington, Georgia. Washington, DC is just one of eighty-eight towns named after our first president. In fact, here's some trivia for you, thirty-one of our fifty states have counties named Washington and New Jersey actually has five townships named Washington."

"You know a lot about this subject," Ania laughed. "Do educators teach such things in the school?"

"Nah." It was his turn to laugh. "I got sidetracked when I was doing an internet search for this town and stumbled across a site about the most common city names and towns in the US." He opened his car door and looked at Ania. "Useless information really."

She looked toward the three story, Queen Anne style Fitzpatrick Hotel where they would spend the night. "This town looks very different than Atlanta, too. Is that why you want to take photos here?"

Luke pointed to the Fitzpatrick. "This small town has some interesting architecture. Like that hotel. It was built with traditional load-bear construction in 1894 but for its exterior they threw a lot of intricate details into the design. There are corner turrets, balconies, stained glass and stone swags yet it maintains a cohesive look. I want to add some of these types of details in unexpected ways on very traditional southern buildings at Magnolia Row. That's what will keep it from being a cookie-cutter community."

"You have a vision. Just like Ruby said." She smiled. "That is a special gift. Not everyone can see beyond what is in front of them. You see the possibilities. That is good, Luke. Very good."

His heart began to pound faster in his chest and he felt a smile building from deep inside him. He wanted to laugh, pull her into his arms and hug her. Her compliment felt better than it should. Hell, these feelings made him feel awkward. He'd never needed to be stroked to feel good about his abilities. He prided himself on not having a big ego, either. Yet, he was thinking he wouldn't mind hearing Ania say a few more nice things about him.

Yeah. He was an idiot.

"Oh Luke, look, there." Ania pointed to a little café on the other side of the courthouse square. "Lucy's Home Cooking Diner. Do you think they serve crispy fried chicken and creamy mashed potatoes with home style gravy?" Her hands waved with an enthusiasm he hadn't seen in her since they met. "I wonder if they use old family recipes? I read that good southern fried chicken needs to be fried in lard. Do you think they have deep fried chicken at the café?"

"Do I look like Colonel Sanders?" He shook his head. "Let's check in to the hotel." Ania reached into the back seat, retrieved his camera bag and the backpack that held his computer and iPad, then jogged around the car to meet him on his side.

"Not very trusting of the natives, are you Ania?" He took the bags from her and slid his gun into his khaki backpack.

"You need these things for work, no?" She looked at him like she didn't understand why he was talking her about trusting the locals.

"Yes, I need them for work. But I also have a really

sophisticated security system on the car." He pressed the key fob and the car beeped twice. "No one is getting into my car without me and everyone else around knowing."

"If they get in, they get your stuff. Noisy alarm or not." She pointed to the bags over her shoulder. "From what I observed about you, work is very important and you have very much of it to do."

He took her hand and led her across the street to the front of the hotel.

Before he reached for the glass lobby door, he released her hand and faced her. Her chin lifted slightly and looked at him, a smile lifted on her lips and in her clear blue eyes. Heat rushed into his chest, hot and instant. All the parts that were male responded to her smile, too.

Oh hell.

He could name this physical reaction to Ania. It was desire. Unwanted desire, yet, powerfully pounding through his body nonetheless. This was a distraction he hadn't considered. Well, not with any real concern. Not until now. Not until his insides felt like he'd sat in a sauna too long and his hands burned to feel her cool, soft bare skin.

Luke clenched his jaws and fisted his hands at his side. This desire was damn inconvenient and it ticked him off. If he acted on what his body wanted, who the hell knew what would happen then. Could it be just a night of pleasure and nothing more? Hell, he didn't have a night to spend enjoying Ania...even if she wanted to. Traveling with her had just gone up ten notches on the distraction meter.

Stay focused on your priorities, Luke.

"You're right, work is very important to me," he said, not trying to hide his anger. "It's why I'm going to ask you to go to your room and stay there while I take care of the things I need to. Watch a movie. Catch up on the news. Read a magazine. Just don't do anything that will stop me from doing my job. Okay? Will you do what I'm asking you to do?"

"No."

"What?"

"No." She started to turn to leave and he grabbed her by the arm and turned her to face him again. "What?"

"That's what I asked you? Don't get angry with me."

"You're the one that sounds angry. I don't talk to you when you are like this."

"The hell you won't." A man walked out of one of the

double hotel doors and looked at Ania. She immediately wrapped her arms around Luke and buried her face in his chest. He knew it was to hide her face from the man staring at her, but having her body pressed against his, sent a new wave of heat and desire burning through his body. Luke nodded to the man who now looked up at him for reassurance that she didn't need him stepping in to help her. Apparently he was convinced Luke wasn't going to hurt her and he walked away down the street.

"I should go to the car now," Ania said, her face still turned into his chest.

Luke gently took her shoulders and pushed her away enough to look at her. "I'm sorry for losing my temper, Ania. I just don't understand why you won't just go to your hotel room and stay inside for the evening."

She blinked. "I can't do that, Luke. I sleep in the car. It is a very beautiful car. The evening is nice. Not too cold."

"The car? I have reservations for two rooms. One for me and one for you."

"I can't afford a room. I don't want to owe you money. I don't know when I will be able to pay you back. I prefer not owing you or anyone else. It is how I got into this trouble in the first place. I will not make that mistake again. I already owe you for the botanical gardens entrance ticket, my new shoes and lunch." She told him to the penny how much that was. "I write it on a papers." She reached into her shirt dress breast pocket and showed him where she was keeping a list on the two small pieces of paper that she'd taken from the notepad in Tanté Izzy and Ruby's hotel room.

He felt like an idiot. This woman was just trying to hold on to something when she had nothing and he was humiliating her further by trying to hide her away in her room because it made his life easier both for work and for dealing with his physical attraction to her.

"Ania, if it isn't safe for my camera, computer and iPad to spend the night in the car, then it isn't safe for you." She looked toward the car, but didn't say anything. "Write the cost of the hotel room on your paper. I'll let you work off what you owe me." She lifted one brow and looked at him. He held up his hands. "Legitimate work."

"Yes. That is good," she smiled and her voice seemed to bounce with her words. "I can be your assistant. I finished in top five percent of my graduation class at the University of

Warsaw in biological science and number two at the Fumenti in Gdansk. I can do the tasks that take you away from your important work. I can organize the papers scattered on the back seat into files. I can..."

"Okay, you're hired," he laughed opening the door to the lobby. 'Biology, huh?"

"I thought I wanted to be a physician." She shook her head. "I changed my mind. I did not like being around sick people."

"That would've been a problem." He smiled. "Tomorrow we'll talk about your employment terms."

"Terms are simple," she said waling into the lobby as he held the door open for her. "You pay my expenses until we get to Cane. And, Luke, I promise to not eat too much."

Chapter Seven

"And, youz is makin' sure Ania is eatin' enough and drinkin' enough, because I don't want her comin' to Cane malnourished because she is too prideful to ask for somethin' to eat. I'm makin' her some shrimp fricassee all da same. Da shrimp are good. Got me some 60-70's coming on Dudley Comeaux's trawl boat. I might let youz have some too if youz been feedin' her good."

"She is eating well. Very well." He smiled. Tanté Izzy had called and said the same thing every morning and evening in the day and a half since they dropped her and Ruby at the airport. He didn't tell her that she was also collecting a salary and getting all of her expenses paid as part of their employment agreement since they started working together. Tanté Izzy would read too much into them working together. Best to keep that part of the trip between him and Ania.

Ania had actually surprised him with how quickly she'd proven that she was an excellent assistant. Luke had intended to just give her things to do so she wouldn't feel bad letting him pay her way. But, she was true to her word and took on all of the time-consuming tasks that he used to do, so he could focus on the new clubhouse designs for Magnolia Row that Trent had emailed to him. Trent also emailed a set of plans for the adjacent pool, tennis courts and playground. So, to get the requested reports completed when Trent wanted them, they had stayed in the Fitzpatrick hotel an extra night.

"Did youz talk to youz sister again about Ania," Tanté Izzy asked, knowing he had spoken to Jen the first night he was in Washington.

"I did, but after talking it to death, we got back to the same conclusions. If Ania isn't willing to press charges against her groom, there isn't anything law officials can do."

Unless Dorek committed a crime.

Luke knew the low-life had. At the botanical gardens he'd assaulted both him and Ania and his intent, as he and his goons chased after them, was to kidnap Ania. Not sure he could prove it, even with surveillance cameras. It'd look like they were all just running through the gardens, maybe not on an exercise jaunt but, nothing that would stick enough for charges to be filed. Or, to get Dorek on a weapons violation, the cameras would've had to see one. That was unlikely. Ania had been the one who actually had the weapon out in the open.

All of that was moot anyways. His gut had warned him not to tell his sister about what happened at the botanical gardens. Jen would've taken the information and been unstoppable in pursuit of justice, not to mention the fact that she'd want to protect her brother and the woman he was traveling with. Protecting people seemed to be something he and his sister both cared about.

Back to square one, unless Ania was willing to press charges. He hated to admit it, but if she was right about Dorek having informants in law enforcement, she probably shouldn't do that...just yet.

"We'z don't need no restrain' order to restrain him, dat's for sure," Tanté Izzy said, ending her statement with a harrumph for finality. "I'ze got to go. Ruby and I are takin' pictures of Ania's weddin' dress at the Sugar Mill Plantation house. It will look like one of dem fancy weddin' magazine pictures. We'll sell it fer sure on eBay."

As soon as he hung up, Ania walked up to the table speaking before she reached him. "Luke, they have *paczkis* here. Have you ever tried paczkis? It is very special in my homeland. We even have a Paczki Day. It is on Fat Thursday, the Thursday before Lent begins." She was wearing a huge smile and a light lavender dress with orange butterflies embroidered randomly over it. The soft, flowy dress made Luke think of the field of monarch butterflies fluttering in a field of sun-kissed lavender that he'd seen near a job site a few years back. The same feeling he had then, filled him now. He wanted to burn the image into his memory so he could recall it later when he needed something beautiful and peaceful to lighten his day.

Without giving much thought to it, he unclipped his phone from his belt and took a photo of Ania standing in front him wearing the short sleeve spring dress and white Keds. She tossed her head back, her ponytail sliding down her back and laughed.

"Why did you photograph me?" she asked

He shrugged, feeling heat rush into his face. *Well that was embarrassing getting caught in a puerile moment.* "So I can show my accountant," he lied. "He'll see the dresses on my credit card and think I've become a cross-dresser."

"He would never think that. You are too much macho to ever wear a dress."

She placed a plate with fresh strawberries, different breads and what she called *paczkis* that she'd gotten from the hotel continental breakfast on the table between them. She sat in the seat across for him. Ania had considered making sure he was well fed as part of her job. Something she did with great excitement when she perused the selections and preparation of their meals in Washington. "I wonder what is inside these paczkis," she said, nudging one of the plates toward him.

"Paczkis? Those are jelly donuts."

She smiled and took a bite of the donut. "Peach. I have never had it with peach before. It is very good." His heart started to beat harder. Damn. It was sexy as hell watching her take slow enthusiastic bites of the jelly donut. Hell, everything she ate was a sensual experience. The way she closed her eyes and let the food rest on her tongue to savor each sweet or savory flavor had him wondering if she'd do the same when she tasted his kisses. Hell, he knew he would as he took his time sliding his tongue over her lush, desirable lips and...

What the hell is wrong with you, Luke? When in the hell did you go from fantasizing about kissing her to thinking of it as a forgone conclusion. He stabbed the scrambled eggs on his plate and swallowed a forkful without tasting it.

Ania-distraction.

Ania-off limits.

"It tastes like the chef used the same homemade peach preserves they serve with the breads," she said, placing a donut on his plate using her fork and knife like tongs. "I love food with a story. The front desk clerk told me an elderly couple who lives north of town makes this preserve for the hotel. Together they pick the peaches in their yard, cook them and put them in glass containers. They have done this for fifty-three years. It makes it extra special, no?" Ania dipped the tip of her spoon into the dark golden preserve she'd placed on her plate and tasted. A drop of the thick jam remained near the bow of her upper lip. Luke nearly groaned out loud as she licked it. "It has a simple taste. They do not use cloves or spices. Just sugar and pectin. But, not too sweet."

He leaned back, placing his fork on his plate. "It's time to go." He folded his arms over his chest.

"May I eat first?"

"I want to be on the road in twenty-minutes," he said on an exhale, regretting his abrupt tone.

"Geez, you got up on the wrong side of the room this morning."

"Bed." He blew out a breath, unable to take his eyes off her beautiful, pink mouth as she gently wiped the corners of it with the edge of the paper napkin as if it was fine linen and she was finishing a formal dinner at a five-star restaurant.

"Bed?"

He leaned forward with his elbows on the table, having a hard time remembering what the hell they were talking about but sure as hell knew he didn't want to talk about beds with Ania.

"Forget it." She sliced a bite of the whole strawberry on her plate using both her fork and knife. She ate everything with a fork and knife, even the pizza they had last night—which she'd dipped into the extra tomato sauce she ordered. Using her fork, of course. Ania looked so damn sophisticated and adorable doing it. He had the sudden urge to steal her utensils so she had to eat with her hands. He was losing his mind.

With his fingers, Luke placed the donut on his plate. "Why do you care so much about the minute details of food? Are you a Foodie? Just knowing it taste good is, well, good enough for me."

She smiled, but he could see by the way her eyes darkened, that his question wasn't a simple one. "Food is my passion and my profession," she said, looking around her as if she wanted to see if anyone was listening. "I am a trained chef."

"Well, hell." He leaned back in his seat. "I should've guessed. Profession. Passion. You taste food like you're making love to it."

She blushed and bit her bottom lip. *Damn, she was so freakin' sexy.*

He cleared his throat. "Thank you for telling me that." He meant it. It may have been the most direct and honest thing she'd shared with him about herself. "Are you a famous chef that I should know because honestly, the only chef I know by name is Chef Boyardee?"

Her laugh was instant. "No. I am not famous at all."

Thank God. That would've complicated things more than they were. "Okay, it is time to move on. I finally can get those photos here in Washington on our way out. I had no idea when I planned the return trip to Louisiana that we'd be here for two days."

"I had no idea I would be in Washington, Georgia. Ever."
She smiled.

"Ania, we need to talk."

"I thought we were," she took a sip of her coffee. God, he
loved when she laughed. It seemed to make everything in the
room brighten, like a curtain had been pulled back and the sun
came shining through. He knew what he had to say would feel
like he'd closed those curtains again.

"I spoke to my sister last night," he began and the way her
smile wilted told him that his serious tone concerned her. "Her
name is Jen. She's an assistant district attorney in Atlanta."

With slow, stiff movements she put her mug down on its
saucer. "You told her about me and my situation?"

"Yes."

"And Dorek?"

"I didn't use your name or his, but, yes, I told her about
your troubles."

"I wish you hadn't done that. It is my problem. My choice
to tell whom I want. Not you." She lifted her mug, but didn't
drink from it.

"Yeah, well, when you got in my car it became my problem
too." He ran his hands through his hair. "Jen thinks you should
file a restraining order against Dorek. I do, too."

"No."

"Hear me out. You owe me that much." He waited for her
to nod before continuing. "I'm concerned about what this,
Dorek, can do to you. I'm not always going to be around to
protect you. And if he is as determined as you claim, and
frankly, as I witnessed, then, this is too dangerous for you to
fight. It falls in the category of needing trained professionals
fighting this battle. We were lucky at the botanical gardens.
Hell, we were lucky to get away the day of your wedding. If it
happens again, we may not be lucky again."

"Maybe not. You are right. So, you go now. I can survive
this on my own." She looked down at her coffee. "You helped
me when I was most in trouble. I appreciate that very much. I
am not stupid or silly woman. I have been smart and careful for
years with a dangerous...situation. I can take care of myself."

"I know you're smart. You have good instincts, are clever
and a quick problem solver. But, you have to be all of those
things all of the time. Dorek just needs to be good at capturing
you one time." He shook his head, not really sure what to say

that would convince her to do what needed to be done. "Ania, let's say for argument sake that you can outsmart Dorek. Do you want to live your life constantly having to focus on that? Do you want to be constantly wondering if he's going to be around the next corner or in the next car that pulls up behind you?" He paused to make sure she understood what he was saying "Don't you want to live in peace, to follow your dreams?"

Her eyes filled with tears and Luke felt like a vice was clamped around his heart.

"Of course I do," she said, her voiced thick with anger and emotion.

"Damn it, Ania, you have options but you are too stubborn to see that," he said, nearly shouting. The breakfast room went silent. He held up his hands and lowered his voice. "I'll meet you at the car in twenty minutes."

He got up and walked away.

Chapter Eight

Three days had passed since Ania and Luke had spoken of getting a restraining order on Dorek. She thought of that conversation often, especially the part when he asked her if she wanted to live in peace, to follow her dreams. That was what kept her up at night when she tried to fall asleep in her lonely hotel room and where her mind drifted to in the quiet times as they drove between the beautiful places Luke stopped to photograph, measure or use for inspiration for the drawings he created. He had not brought it up again, and she certainly did not either. She wondered if he thought about it as she did. She knew he had to think of it at least a little when she heard him speaking to his sister, telling her his hands were tied.

Ania's hands were tied, too.

She learned much about Luke and his passion for his work in the days that followed. She enjoyed the way he spoke of the homes and public spaces he wanted to build in the Magnolia Row community; the way he spoke with fondness and admiration of the individual employees he had working with him; and the way he treated her with such honor and respect. Yet, nothing was more telling of his kind and good character than discovering a jar of peach preserves when she got into the car after their upsetting conversation at the Fitzpatrick Hotel.

Ania fell in love with Luke at that moment.

Nerves stirred in her belly now as they had when she first realized the truth of her feelings. It was the same nerves she had felt when she boarded the plane to leave her home in Poland and travel to America for new opportunities. She wasn't that naïve dreamer that she was then, but she wasn't an emotionless zombie either. No, she understood that there was no hope for her love to be anything but her private joy and torture, but wow, it felt as fresh and exciting as the blooming spring after a long, cold. winter.

Ania understood that Luke was a kind man. It was part of the reason she fell in love with him. She would never confuse his kindness as love, though. It was enough for her to just love him and appreciate his good intent toward her. Like when he'd surprised her after their amazing visit to historic Savannah by heading west to attend the Glennville Sweet Onion Festival. He told her that he wanted to bring her to the Festival because he knew how much she enjoyed experiencing America folk life and regional food. Hearing him say that gave her the tingling thrill of discovering that her schoolgirl crush liked her a little. That excitement continued as they tasted the incredible festival food and as he waited for her to discuss how each dish featuring the Vidalia onion was prepared with the festival volunteers. And, as they rode the vintage carousel with the menagerie of white horses, bold zebras and open mouth lions, his smile sparked easily, making her heart feel as light as magical gossamer fairy's wings. Never in Ania's life had she enjoyed an evening of such abandon and whimsy with a man whose thoughtfulness and friendly companionship made her forget the hardship of her past and the despair of her today.

"Did you like Pebble Hill Plantation," he asked on Tuesday as they drove on Interstate-10, heading west away from Thomasville, Georgia.

"Very much. I can see why you wanted to go there. Like you told me, it is a very good model for your Magnolia Row."

"I like how nothing feels crowded on the property, yet it feels special and part of life there." His eyes were on the road and hidden behind his dark glasses, but she knew they would be bright and clear as he spoke of his dreams.

"I like how nothing looked too new. In America, there is much polish and perfection. It is nice to see some iron-oxide on the barn roof, and some wear on the stone from years of rain and wind."

He glanced at her, his smooth lips lifted in a smile. "Ania, that is a very good point. We should make sure we have some buildings that look as if they have been there for years."

"Yes," she clapped her hands. "I loved that iron-oxide roof on the shed near the vegetable garden. It was so beautiful with its gray wooden walls and red-orange-and brown roof doors adjacent to it."

He laughed. "Iron-oxide is rust."

She shrugged. "I thought rust was a color not a chemical reaction."

"It is both." Luke turned to look at her for a brief moment. Ania felt the intensity of his gaze through the barrier of his dark lenses and his integrity.

She had felt it before. She had seen it too.

Over the days they had been together she sometimes

caught him staring at her, with his intoxicating, sensual eyes. She felt his desire as she did now, as if he was physically caressing her. It left her breathless and wanting. But, he did nothing more than look. She did nothing to encourage him, although she wanted to. But, what he wanted and what she wanted were not the same. What could be between them would last only a short time. She had to leave America.

And Luke.

If they gave into their desires and made love, she knew with every fiber of her being that when she departed, it would break her heart.

"We have about another hour and a half before we reach the condo where we are staying," he said, his voice deeper than it was before.

"With a kitchen?"

"Yes, a kitchen and a view of the Gulf of Mexico."

She sat up. "Oh, this is exciting. I have never seen the oceans around America."

"You're kidding?" He shook his head. "Of course, you're not. Have you been anywhere other than Atlanta since coming to the states?"

"No. Just Atlanta. I didn't even fly into any other American airport coming here. That is funny, no?"

Luke didn't answer. He reached over and squeezed her hand. "I'm glad you're getting to see some of the country."

"Thank you, Luke. I know our trip started as an escape from Dorek. But, it has turned into so much more." She looked away so he would not see the sadness she felt for falling in love with him, when she had so much to be thankful for.

"I should've thought of taking you to the Atlantic Ocean when we were in Savannah. We were only about twenty minutes away."

"Oh, no, do not feel regrets." How did she tell him that everything had been perfect? "I enjoyed the Historic District, the Mercer-Williams House and oh, the River Street Market along the Savannah river was incredible. Plus, the trip to the Sweet Onion Festival..." She clasped her hands in front of her. "I couldn't want more. Your work and your thoughtfulness has been very...oh, I don't know the word..." She looked at Luke, her eyes stinging with unshed tears. "*Kocham cie.*"

"*Kocham cie*, huh?" he laughed.

She wished with all her heart that he wasn't just parroting the words, and that he knew their meaning, and really meant them.

Yes, I love you.

Ania closed her eyes and pretended to fall asleep. Even having to survive the pain of unrequited love, Ania knew was not as bad as living in the home of an awful mob member and working in his restaurant with no means of escape. She was a prisoner in the home of the man she thought would help her. Soon she would be free to return to Poland, if the United States government didn't imprison too.

When she heard the blinker ticking an hour later, she sat up.

"Do you smell the salt air?"

She inhaled deeply. "Oh, yes. It is wonderful. And warm." She looked on both sides of the road at the large fields where green tractors were forming rows to plant their crop. "What do they grow here?"

"Those are cotton fields. They are harvested in July."

"We don't have crops back home but we have a very big cotton textile industry"

Luke touched her hand. It felt warm, heavy and familiar. "Ania, do you have family back home?"

She shook her head. "Not close family." She turned her hand and interlocked her fingers with his. "I have no siblings. I was an only child. My father and mother are deceased. My father died of a *udar mózgu.*"

"I'm sorry, I don't speak Lithuanian. What is that?"

She hated not telling him she was from Poland, but reminded herself that it was for his own good. "I do not know the exact medical words. I think you call it a brain stroke."

"How old was he?"

"Fifty-five. My mother died five months later of a broken heart."

"Is that possible?"

"Yes," she said with certainty. "Her health declined from the day she held him in her arms in the fields of our farm where they had been working together. I was off at university when I got the news."

"That is difficult. I understand. I lost my family in one horrible accident." He squeezed her hand and she felt his pain in that simple gesture. "A plane crash while on vacation in Alaska. My mother, two aunts, two uncles and several cousins. I was home starting my construction company. My sister, Jen was in law school."

"I am so sorry for your sadness and loss. It must have been very difficult. What about your father? Was he in the plane too?"

"No. He was gone from our lives before my sister was born." He spoke with so little emotion about his father that Ania would have thought it did not matter, except for the muscle that tightened in his jaw. "His choice. His loss."

He stopped at traffic light at an intersection to a four lane highway. He put on his blinker to turn left. "So you came to the states after they passed?"

She looked at him, wandering how much she should tell him. If he knew too much about her, then Dorek and his father would consider him a threat too. "Yes. I was in the final days of my post-university studies at Fumenti to become a chef when my father died," she began, carefully choosing her words. "I got my certificate of completion, but did not attend any ceremony. I was already back to my village. I cared for my mother until her death." She lifted her wrist to show him her medal. "My mother had given this to me for protection. It is Our Lady of *Czestochowa*. It is very special to me. My mother said she loves me eternally just as our mother Mary loved her son."

She closed her eyes and placed her hands back on her lap. Luke touched her cheek gently with the back of his hand trying to soothe her. "That is a good memory for you to have." The light changed and he turned onto the four-lane highway. "What made you decide to come to the US?"

"My godfather invited me to come to work for him and live with his family in Atlanta." She shrugged. "I had just sold our six-hectare farm. That is about fifteen American acres. I had to use the money to pay mortgages, bills and well, you understand, the expenses a potato harvest would have helped with. I had nothing left except much sadness in my heart. I think, it would be good to go to a new place and start new memories."

Ania looked up at the billboards lining the road reading like a tourist brochure. She was glad that there was something else that they could speak of, other than her history. "There is much to do here," she said, happy to have something else to talk about. "A zoo, water park, restaurants." She inhaled deeply, the scent of the salt air was stronger. "I am glad we have not just stayed on the interstate."

"Life begins at the off-ramp." He smiled. "I read that somewhere."

"I believe it does."

They drove over the Intracoastal Waterway, passed a beautiful condo and shopping development that Luke called The Wharf, where he pointed out the huge Ferris wheel that was so high you could see the Gulf of Mexico when you reached the crest. There were large yachts in the nearby marina and lots and lots of palm trees. Ania felt she was on an exotic island and she hadn't even gotten to the beach.

"We will just make it in time to see the sunset," Luke said as they turned onto another road and saw the ocean ahead of them.

"Oh, my God. This is beautiful." Ania started chattering about the white, sugar sand beach and the calm turquoise water. She pointed to palm trees that were taller than and as straight as columns on some of the grandest plantation homes they saw. And, she looked up at the tall condominium buildings with deep blue windows and wide balconies facing the ocean.

Luke laughed out loud at her silly ramblings and she laughed too. "Now, can you repeat everything you just said in English?" he asked.

"Oh no. I thought I was talking in English."

They drove over a bridge, where they saw a state park to the right with a couple holding hands as they walked on a meandering boardwalk over sea grass and sand. Three minutes later, they were turning into a shell parking lot in front of a light blue, three story building with milk white trim. The beach was behind it.

"Is this it?" She unbuckled her safety belt and stood, the wind blowing from the gulf whipped her hair behind her. "I must be in heaven."

"I always think so when I'm here." His eyes remained steady on hers.

"You come often?" He shook his head but his smile was filled with a sort of satisfaction too. Oh, God. Ania had the sudden knowledge that she knew why. "This whole condo-complex is yours, no?"

"Yeah." He looked at the beautiful building sighed. "I rent the seven units on the second and third floors. The top one is mine. I don't rent it. I want it to be available for whenever I can get away."

Luke's phone began to ring. He looked at her, then the screen of his phone. He tossed it onto her seat. "I don't want to miss the sunset. Let's go."

Ania couldn't believe he had done that. It was probably his office calling. They usually called around this time. Luke got out of the car and came around and opened her door. Ania stepped out, picked up his phone and tucked it into the side pocket of the white, linen dress she was wearing.

Luke made fast work of unlocking the condo door to the top floor unit using the keypad. He grabbed her hand and pulled her through a short foyer, past a large living room-kitchen combination, out to the balcony facing the Gulf. There were no words grand enough to describe the even warmth of the sun on her face and arms; the rhythmic sound of the crashing waves on the shore; the scent of the crisp sea air carried on the spirited breeze; the visual pleasure of the fresh, clean colors that looked like every beautiful painting of the seaside she had seen; and the joy singing through her body from being able to share this with Luke.

As if he heard her unspoken words, he turned her to face him and looked down at her. Taking off his sunglasses, he tossed them onto a nearby table. Ania didn't wait for him to pull back—hold back this time—as his dilated eyes settled on hers. Nor did she allow herself to think of all the reasons she shouldn't kiss him. She grabbed the loose fabric of his soft, black polo shirt at his waist and pulled him to her. Luke sucked in a breath.

"Ania," he said her name like a warning.

Lifting up onto the toes of her sneakers, she pressed her lips to his.

"Ania." This time her name sounded like a surrender. Luke sighed as his mouth slid over hers, warm, wet and wonderful. He filled his hand with her hair and pressed his other hand against the center of her back, pulling her tighter against his hard, male body. Ania smiled with her lips against his.

"Holy crap." He growled and his tongue swept along the seam of her lips. Ania opened her mouth to him. She would not hold back anything with Luke. She wanted to experience him with all of her senses. She wanted every texture, taste, scent, nuance to burn in the synapses of her brain so she could close her eyes and dream of it when he was no longer with her.

Ania felt the smooth stroke of his tongue with hers as her body heated and melted into his. Her hands slid up his sides to his thick, muscular shoulders, then around his neck where his wind disheveled hair curled around her fingers. He growled from the pleasure of her touching him, emboldening her to touch him more. She stepped tighter against him, and nibbled on his bottom lip, then his chin and back to his mouth.

Luke's hands slid down her back, onto her bottom, pulling her harder against him. Ania felt his desire and smelled the intoxicating scent of soap, mint gum and masculinity. The sea, the beach, the man. No time, no place, no other person could be more perfect for Ania.

"Take me to bed," she said, her mouth a breath from his. Luke lifted her into his arms.

"Are you sure, darlin'?"

"Yes." She kissed him again, this time with the all the passion she felt from deep within her heart. If she went to prison for immigration violations, if she should die at Dorek's hands, then she would go knowing she had fully loved this man who had captured her heart.

Luke carried her inside. It was such a strange sensation to give over all control to another person. But she trusted Luke to take care of her. He'd been doing so since they met. He pulled back the blankets and gently placed her on the bed. Ania felt the cool, cotton sheets against her legs where her dress had lifted and left her legs bare. Luke knelt on the bed next to her and looked at her, his hazel eyes only visible as a narrow, light ring around his black pupils. He pulled his shirt off and tossed it behind him. Ania had never seen him without his shirt before. She knew he was strong, fit, but she had no idea his abdomen muscles were so defined.

He eased down on the bed alongside of her and ran his fingers along the length of her arm. "You are so beautiful, soft."

She shivered. He lifted her hand and kissed her palm, taking his time as his mouth slid a sensual path up her arm before sliding the fabric of her dress off her shoulder and kissing her exposed flesh. His mouth moved lower to kiss the top swell of her breasts. Ania's head fell back and Luke unlaced the ribbon holding the front of her dress together. Tender kisses whispered where the material opened, exposing her. Ania couldn't lay still as all the parts of her that made her a woman, felt anxious, wanting.

She lifted her torso, kissed Luke on his chest and feathered her fingers over his nipples. Silk over steel. He growled and fell onto his back, pulling her on top of him. His hand slid down to her thigh, pulling her dress up to her waist. She moved her center over his, feeling how much he desired her. Luke squeezed her bottom, pulling her tighter against him. Ania's legs fell open, instinctively, naturally. Love now flowed with need, both were the same. Both were powerful and hungry. Consuming.

Luke's mouth found hers again, as his thumbs hooked on the edge of her panties and drew them down to her knees. Ania, kicked them off the rest of the way, then slid off the bed and stood. He tucked a pillow behind his head. His hand resting over his heart.

Oh Luke is your heart beating as hard as mine?

"Take it off, Ania. Slowly." His voice was so deep, so sexy, Ania, shivered although heat burned from her core. She turned her back to him, grabbed the hem of her dress and looked at him over her shoulder as she lifted the dress, exposing her bare bottom to him. He sucked in a breath, his muscles tightening. He lifted his finger and motioned for her to lift it higher. She did, pulling it over her head, clutching it to her chest as she turned to face him.

"I changed my mind. Too slow." Luke yanked the dress from her and tossed it onto the floor with a thump because of the cell phone in her pocket. He sucked in his breath, looking at her naked, exposed body with hooded eyes. Ania felt so vulnerable, but something in Luke's gaze made her feel powerful too. "The glow of the setting sun is sneaking in along the sides of the drapes, making you look like you are painted in gold. Beautiful."

He stood in front of her, his eyes steady on hers as his fingers touched her erect nipples as if they were fragile glass. She inhaled, and Luke's mouth covered one nipple taking his time, tasting as if she were sweet Paczki just taken from the oven. With such tenderness and care, he lifted her into his arms, and eased her onto the bed before settling on his side next to her. His hand slid down her belly and paused. Ania covered his hand, and eased it to where they both wanted it to be. His fingers stoked the fire within her until the flames flared hot and bright, Ania reached between them, unbuttoned his jeans, slid the zipper down.

"Ania..." His words were lost, either because he didn't say them or she didn't hear them as she lifted her hips with the rhythm he began. Luke rolled onto his back, pulled his pants off, reached into this wallet for a condom and returned to her.

Now it was Ania's turn to look. He was perfect, virile and for a time, hers. This was going to happen. With the man she loved.

Luke slipped on the condom, eased on top of her, spreading

her legs apart. He kissed her hard, with a passion she had never felt from a man before, one that she never believed existed. Then, they took the next step, the one that had eluded her since her one experience while in college, the one she wanted to share now with the man she loved. Luke moved inside of her and they quickly found the rhythm of the surf they heard through the closed windows. Ania felt that magical thing she heard her college friends describe, build inside her. Little sounds of pleasure slid over her lips as Luke's breath grew heavier, deeper. Then, everything seemed to explode in a powerful release that left her vibrating. Luke called out her name as his body went still.

He collapsed on her, taking some of his weight onto the arms that were bent at her sides.

He kissed her on the neck with such sweet, tenderness and care. Ania wrapped her arms around him and held on...while she could.

Chapter Nine

Luke sat in the kitchen and couldn't muster any guilt or remorse for having the best sex of his life. Yeah, he should've fought against the hard crush of desire consuming him every time he looked at seductive Ania, but he was glad he hadn't. It had been great. Both times. It would be great a third and fourth time too. Even now, his arms burned to wrap around her narrow waist, pull her yielding body against his chest and...Whoa! Time to put on the brakes. He had work to do. Ania had proved to be the distraction he feared but hadn't anticipated. Damn, but she was a satisfying distraction.

"Smells good," he said, inhaling deeply, rubbing his hand across the front of the faded blue t-shirt that he wore over his old navy blue athletic shorts. His stomach growled reminding him he hadn't eaten since lunch, as he took in the powerful scents of garlic, onion, vinegar and who the hell knew what else Ania was using to cook. He turned on his laptop that he'd set up on the cream granite bar and settled on the cushioned counter height stool.

Emails. He had to answer his emails.

But, his eyes settled on Ania chopping bright purple cabbage at the kitchen island instead. It reminded him of how she looked on the swing in the botanical gardens. A living sculpture.

She was beautiful in her rumpled white dress with the tan dishtowel tossed over her shoulder and her long, dark wavy hair haphazardly gathered on top of her head. Just as she'd been when she was surrounded by the rich colors of the blooming flowers on that swing, here she was cast against the intense purple of the cabbage, vibrant orange of the mandarins and deep green of the parsley spread out on the counter like paint on an artist's palette. It was eye-sex for the senses. And what made it all that much more special for him was that it was in his space, the one he'd built with his own hands.

When he used a hammer, nail, grout and sweat to create this kitchen, he thought of the sugar sand beach for the color of his white shaker cabinets; the glimmering, turquoise gulf for his glass tile backsplash; and the weathered boardwalks over the sand dunes for his wood floors.

What he never considered was how a determined woman would blend into that space too.

Coming here with her was a big friggin' mistake.

Now, every time he came to his retreat on the beach, he'd think of Ania in the kitchen cooking dinner for them...and of her in his bed. Would the memory be good or bad? Something to enjoy or long for because it could never happen again?

Luke looked down pretending to read his emails, but his eyes kept returning to Ania. It surprised him how easily and happily she moved in the kitchen. The way she held the nine-inch knife while chopping the cabbage with one hand as she gently gripped the food with a protective bend of her fingers with the other, told him she took cooking very seriously. Her eyes sparkled with enjoyment as her body vibrated with energy as she reached into the sink to her left for more vegetables.

Dear Lord...more vegetables?

"You're not making anything too healthy and weird, are you?" he asked, as she began slicing something that looked like a giant scallion "What's that?"

"Leeks." She did a one-eighty to stir the pot on the large six-burner stove he'd only ever used to scramble eggs.

"What's in the pot?"

"The first course. Dill pickle soup."

"Sounds like weird food to me."

"Oh. You will like it. It is an old family recipe'."

Didn't she have an old family recipe that resembled plain ole' meatloaf and mashed potatoes?

She returned to the island and peeled two oranges before tossing them into a bowl with the cabbage, leeks, and pecans. "You watch me too much," she told him as she poured the dressing she created with red wine vinegar, olive oil, honey, Dijon mustard and lemon juice. "Do your work."

"You know that salad qualifies as too healthy and weird." He smiled and when she smiled back his heart started to pound in his chest. Must be the lower barometric pressure from the thunderstorm that was gathering off the coast. Luke looked at her slightly parted lips. Kissing those warm, soft lips created a thunderstorm of desire all the way into the marrow of his bones. That's because she was such a good kisser, he told himself, and because she was cooking for him. There was a reason old-timers said the way to a man's heart was through his stomach.

...and through Ania's lips.

Not his heart, he reminded himself. His anatomy that responded to Ania was nowhere near his heart.

He felt Ania's eyes on him like she'd actually touched him to wake him from a dream. But, when he looked at her light blue eyes, they seemed to turn as gray as the storm clouds hanging low over the gulf. His breath caught in his lungs. There was so much dark emotion there. Why? What was wrong?

Luke stood, started to move toward her but she held up her hand. "No. No. No. Do not fall in love with me, Luke Marcelle. Do not do it."

"Love? Are you crazy? Can't a guy enjoy a healthy bit of lusting without a woman thinking that's he's gone all chick flicks on her." She nodded, but he could see it in her eyes, she didn't believe him. "I'm serious Ania, there are plenty 'L' words I can think of to describe what I'm feeling—lust, like, lucky..."

"Lying." She waved like she was swatting a fly or shooing him away. That gesture felt worse than it should have, and that surprised the hell out of Luke. "I do not want to talk about it. I did not say you were in love with me, just to not fall in love with me. We are an impossibility. Did I say that correctly?"

"You said it correctly. That is a very good word to describe us. I'm glad you realize it. It takes the weight off my shoulders."

"I know that idiom," she said, not smiling. "Here is one for you in my language—*rzucać grochem o ścianę.*

Luke laughed. Her words sounded soft, gentle and rhythmic, but the little sassy shake of her head made what she was saying sassy. "Did you say O' Suzanna? Because if you did, I know that song."

"Nie," she laughed. "The idiom is—throw peas to the wall—meaning it is useless to argue with someone who cannot be convinced what is right. The person who is..."

"Stubborn?" he pointed to his chest. "Me? Are you calling me stubborn?" He got up and rushed toward her. She took off to race around the other side of the island, he took a step pretending he was going to her side, but quickly changed directions and caught her in his arms as she tried to run in the other direction.

"Yes. You are stubborn. But you are determined too. I do not really know the difference between the two words." She shoved at his chest, but he felt there wasn't much effort behind it, so he pulled her tighter against him and kissed her.

His phone began to ring. "Here's another 'L' word for you, Ania," he said, unclipping his phone at his waist. "Lethal. That was a lethal kiss." He looked at the screen and answered the phone. "Hey Jen."

"Are you sitting down and is she there with you right now?"

"No and yes." He didn't like the breathy, anxious sound of her voice. He pictured his sister twirling her finger in the short layers of her light brown hair as her hazel eyes were looking out the window of her messy office where she was undoubtedly working late.

"Well go somewhere she can't hear us talking and sit down."

He motioned to Ania that he was going outside as he walked to the beachside door. Before he closed it behind him, he looked at her as she opened the oven door. Luke had a feeling he would see her differently when he came back inside.

"I'm outside, alone." He leaned on the balcony rail. The salty sea swept breeze was cool and pleasant. He could always count on the breeze feeling good against his cheeks and in his hair when he stood on his balcony looking out at the timeless gulf. No matter what his sister had to say about Ania, this would remain the same.

"Do you know who you're traveling across the southern United States with?" She exhaled. "Of course you don't. It's why I'm calling you."

Luke waited for Jen to say what she knew. There was no reason for him to respond.

"She's wanted for questioning by the FBI and US Attorneys' office. Plus, US Customs and Immigration Enforcement is looking for her for a visa overstay. Apparently there was an ICE agent at her wedding to witness the blessed event. That's pretty damn unusual. Why were they there when there are almost a half-million people roaming around our country on overstay visas? Oh, wait. Could it be because the FBI and US attorney's office put out the alert on her?"

"What the hell is going on?"

"Ania Darsk ..."

"Darsk, huh? She told me her last name was Mitchell."

"No big surprise. She knows she'd be deported if she was discovered because of the overstay at the least. I'm not sure she knows the FBI wants to question her though. I suspect she might since she disappeared after her fiancé, Dorek Kaminski, was charged with first degree murder of Mark Perdek. They never recovered the gun he used to shoot Perdek, point blank in the head, but they found his body in the landfill."

Never found the murder weapon? Luke thought of Dorek's gun Ania had taken from him at the botanical gardens that Luke had dismantled and thrown away throughout Georgia. Crap, that was a stupid move.

He focused on what his sister was saying. He'd tell her about the gun later. "Perdek was in deep-cover for the FBI trying to make the case against Polish-American organized crime in Atlanta. In his last report, he said that Dorek was getting suspicious of him. Hell, I shouldn't have told you that. You can never, ever repeat it."

"Polish-American organized crime? I had no idea there was such a thing. And the murder of an FBI agent." *Holy crap. Dorek wasn't just some crazed, possessive groom trying to get his bride back.*

"Oh, there is such a thing. The Polish mob is real."

"Ania told me that Dorek wouldn't give up chasing her down because he considered her a threat to him. Do you know if she was a witness to the murder? Did she see Dorek murder Perdek or does she have damning information about it or something else that could send him away for life? What in the hell kind of stuff is Dorek involved in?"

"RICO stuff and we suspect worse, although the evidence against him for the Perdek murder seems circumstantial." Jen sounded much calmer than Luke felt. "Kaminski and about a dozen others are under investigation by the FBI. They were building a pretty solid case against these guys with their informant on the inside."

"How is Ania involved in all of this?"

"I don't know, exactly. It's all hush-hush. But, I have a friend," she lowered her voice as she spoke into the phone, "Luke, like the info on Perdek, I have some real inside info here that you can't share with Ania on the chance she's more friend than foe to these thugs."

"You have my word."

"What I learned is that charges are being filed tomorrow by the US Attorney General under RICO for Dorek, his father, and twenty-six others. You can't say anything to Ania in case she shares that info with them and they flee."

"Jen, I'm having a hard time digesting all of this. I feel like I landed in an Eliot Ness movie." He sat. The chair felt cold and damp against his exposed legs. "Let's just talk about Ania.

What's her involvement with the Polish Mob?"

"This is what I found out about her from being allowed to read the informants' reports. Ania was a chef at the Kaminski restaurant. The restaurant was the meeting place for their boss—Henryk Tworkov, the head of the mob. Dorek's father, Lech, appears not to be hard-core into the criminal activities, but he did allow them to use his restaurant as a meeting place. For keeping his mouth shut he got occasional cash bonuses. Dorek is another matter. He's a soldier. Anyway, back to Ania. All I read was that she was there working in the restaurant. She's an immigrant from Poland. She's good at her job and, as far as they know, didn't socialize with anyone that came to, or worked in the restaurant. She kept to herself. But, the kicker is, she lived with the Kaminski's—Lech, his wife, another son and Dorek." She paused a moment, he heard her chair squeak like she was rocking in it.

"She lived with them, Luke. She had to know what was going on. She might've even been an associate, you know an errand girl for the mob. Maybe she was a courier. She had to be involved or why in the hell did she stay?"

"I can't see it," he said, thinking about the Ania he knew that kept a ledger of all of the money she intended to pay back of what he'd spent to feed, clothe and house her. "Unless she's been playing me." He thought of her taking the gun in the botanical shed from Dorek's man, tossing it out the window and how she never made the mistake of telling him anything he shouldn't know.

"You know, my answer to that is probably. But, I'm as jaded as they come."

"So, she's wanted for questioning. Any idea if the FBI is trying to build a case against her?"

"I don't know. But, I can tell you that a wife can't be forced to testify against her husband...and vice versa."

"Marrying an American is also a path to citizenship," Luke countered.

"If those were her reasons for marrying, why did she run? Not our problem to figure out. She needs to come in for questioning. At the very least the police can protect her."

"She said Dorek has friends everywhere, including in the police department. She doesn't trust anyone."

"Apparently, she trusts you." Jen's chair squeaked again. "Luke, she's mixed up with some very, very dangerous criminals. She may be one herself. That puts you in the middle of it." She lowered her voice again. "Look, big brother, you've got to dump her. You're a wanted man too, now. You're harboring an illegal alien. It's a violation of the law to conceal, harbor or shield from detection a person who is in the US without a legal status. Luke, this is serious. You could go to jail for five years."

"How long can you go to jail if you destroyed and disposed of a murder weapon?"

Chapter Ten

"Luke?" Ania opened the door leading the balcony and looked outside. He was sitting, looking out toward the gulf, his phone sitting on the table next to him. He didn't turn to look at her. She sat in the chair next to him but didn't say anything. His body language was different than when he left the kitchen, something had profoundly changed.

But what? And why?

What had he and sister discussed to cause this? Or what had he battled in his mind to cause it? She was afraid to find the answer. Her heart squeezed painfully in her chest.

"Dinner is ready," she said, looking for a neutral topic to get him to talk to her.

"Later." He turned and looked at her, the wind tossing his hair over his forehead. He got up, walked to the balcony railing and gripped it with both hands. His forearm muscles flexed as he squeezed the wooden rail tighter and he looked at the choppy gulf. "I'm so furious with myself for letting us get to this point."

She sucked in a breath as if she'd been struck. *No, Luke do not regret taking me to bed.* It was beautiful. "Luke, I am not sorry for our beautiful joining. It was perfect. Please do not have regrets about it. I do not. It was very special to me."

His head came up and his feet down. "Yeah, it was good." He stood, walked to the closed gate near the stairs that led to the beach. "But I can sure think of a lot of reasons it shouldn't have happened." He turned to face her. His eyes, hard to read in the dark corner where he stood.

She walked over and touched the side of his cheek. He turned away, opened the gate and walked down onto the empty beach. Ania hesitated a moment, wondering if she should get her shoes, but decided to just followed him.

When they reached where the sand was wet and cool from the crashing waves dying on the beach, she touched his arm. "I do not like you being angry with me. It makes me hurt inside."

"Excuse me if I'm not feeling sympathetic." He looked up to the starless sky, where dark clouds blew overhead blocking out all light. The only way they could see around them was because of the bright white curl of the wave, light seafoam, and lights from the condo behind them. "Like I said before, I'm not angry with you. I'm angry with me. I should've worked harder to learn what in the hell was going on with you from the beginning. But, I didn't want to get involved in something that would take me away from the Magnolia Row bid. I should've realized that the very people I was trying to protect at my company by not getting too involved in your problems, are the ones I'm hurting now because of it."

"You were right to not ask more then. I would not have told you anyway."

"Of course not. You wanted to use me to do your bidding. Whatever the hell that is."

"If you want to know what the hell it is now, ask me." Ania squatted down, grabbed a handful of the wet, fine sand and let it flow through her fingers. "My life is very much like this sand. When it is wet, it is easier to walk on and when it is dry, it is soft, and each step you take makes you sink until it so very hard to walk. I have lived in the soft sand a very long time. I am very tired of being there. All I have thought about was pushing through it until I reached the wet, packed sand."

He blew out a breath, and sat on the dry beach. "I'm damned if I know everything, and damned if I don't." He patted the sand next to him. "I've lied to myself about many things since you hopped in my car. One being that not knowing about your life would keep me from caring. If I didn't know about your personal struggles or vulnerabilities, then we could just remain impersonal strangers. Well, it didn't work. I do care about you."

He said it like he was angry that he cared and that made Ania want to cry.

She sat next to him and buried her bare feet in the soft, cool sand. She wanted to hold his hand, feel his warm, strong palm pressed against hers. He clearly would not want that. She felt so alone...again even though he sat next to her. Dear Lord, this loneliness was ripping her heart in two as it hadn't before– and she had been alone for a long time.

Love. Love did this.

"Did your sister tell you my story?" she asked, pulling her knees to her chest.

"What difference does that make? Do you want to know what she said so you don't have to tell me more than I know? Do you plan to lie to me by omission, again?"

She watched a small crab dart ahead of the crashing wave. "I do not want to involve you."

"Too late."

She swallowed so hard it hurt. "I am here in America on a working visa. I got it because I am a chef, with very good credentials." Ania closed her eyes and saw herself in the kitchen at Fumeti. She was so young, carefree, and happy then. "I told you this, but I will explain more. I loved culinary school very much. I was happy there and enjoying my final three days to completion when I got a call my father had died. As I told you, my mother became very heart broken. She did not eat or sleep from the day he died until she passed away five months later, the day of their wedding anniversary." She had to pause a moment. She was breathing much too hard. Her head felt light, her stomach heavy. The sadness of that day, that time still felt current, painful. "It was a very bad thing. I was young in my thoughts although I was twenty-three, I was so...what is the word? So, full of expectations that life would be good and successful. Happy. I was on my path to help my parents. It was my hope and plan to do that. Then, my dear father was gone and the mother I knew—so full of life—lost her desire to live that very day too. I died some that day, too. My dreams were so connected to them."

She glanced at Luke, he was still looking out at the ocean. Was he listening? Did he know how hard it was for her to tell him this?

"I am sorry for your loss," he said, his voice deep, solemn.

"Thank you," She hugged her legs tighter, as her dress flapped around her calves in the wind as much of her hair was blown free from its ponytail. "Not only did I mourn for them," she continued, "I had to immediately tend to their desperate finances. They had worked so hard in the fields, needing the harvest to get them through another year. But on their death, the mortgage was called. You may remember that I told you, I had to sell the farm, their home, the happy place I grew up." She rested her cheek on her knees and looked toward Luke. "I had no work, and no direction. I lost my desire and hope during my mourning and while dealing with the burdens of life. I could not have the storybook dream of caring for my parents with my culinary success. I lived in my physically painful feelings." She touched the medal, hanging from the ribbon bracelet at her wrist, that her mother had given her.

"So that's when you took your godfather's offer to come to

the US?"

"Do you mind if we walk? I need to move."

Luke stood and automatically extended his hand to hers. It didn't feel like a gesture of friendship or love. It was just done out of respect, habit. He stepped onto the wet sand, and she did too. Would telling him the rest of her story be as easy as walking on hard sand. A larger wave crashed onto the beach and flowed forward, covering her feet with the chilly clear water. She stopped. Closed her eyes. Trying to memorize every bit of the feel of the gulf water gliding on her toes as it returned from where it came from. She looked at Luke who had paused to wait for her.

"We walk," she said, trying to gather her thoughts to finish telling him about her life. "As I said before to you on drive, my godfather invited me to come to America. I did not remember him well, but I did know who he was. He learned from his family in my village that I was living with a friend until I could get a job and earn enough money to get my own apartment." She shook her head. "He offered me to come to America to live with his family in his townhouse. He said it was his duty to help me. I felt a little hope again. I was going to the land of opportunity to start fresh."

"You were sad and lost. He took advantage of you," Luke said, and her heart skipped a beat. Maybe he would understand, not hate what she would say. "You went to another continent to a man you didn't really know. Didn't it ever dawn on you that might be a problem?"

Maybe, he was less understanding than she hoped. "No. He was my godfather. He promised before God at my baptism to take the place of my parents if something happened to them. He was doing that."

"Godparents give you cool gifts, they don't adopt an adult godchild."

Her face flamed with heat and anger. "I am Catholic, Luke." She didn't care that she was raising her voice. Who would hear, the crabs? "We take our vows during the holy sacraments very seriously." She started to walk faster. "He arranged for my passage, my visa, everything. I had nothing. He offered me something. I was going to work in his restaurant, doing what I loved. I was going to be his head chef."

"Did your godfather treat you well? Did you feel you owed him? Did you do anything he asked because he saved you?"

She stopped turned to face him and shoved him hard. He

stumbled back. She advanced on him. "What are you saying? Are you saying I did unnatural things with him? How dare you?"

When she went to shove him again, he grabbed her wrists. "No Ania. I wasn't inferring that. I was talking about you working for the Polish mob out of gratitude for him. Did you work for the Polish mob?" He released her.

Ania felt her knees weaken. She had to fight to keep from falling to the beach. Hearing him ask her that, made the blood drain to her feet. Did he think she was capable of that evil? Is that the kind of woman he thought she was? Didn't he know her as she knew him, although they hadn't shared the details of their lives?

"No. I am not in the mob."

Luke lifted her chin to look into her eyes. "When did you find out that Lech Kaminski was in the mob?"

So he knew her godfather's name. It should not surprise her that his sister discovered it and told him. "About a week after I arrived." Tears filled her eyes. "I felt betrayed. Sick. I asked him about a conversation I heard from some customers as I served them the Golabki I had made special with fresh cabbage. These men came every day that first week. They called themselves *Dzika Armia* – Wild Boar Army. A very dangerous animal in Poland. They spoke openly in front of me, but in English. I wasn't sure I had heard their conversation accurately. I thought it was because my English was not good. But, then I heard them speaking in Polish about hurting someone who had not paid for protection."

"What did your godfather tell you?"

"To mind my own business. Do the job he brought me over to do. That they were named Wild Boar Army for a reason." She bit her bottom lip, remembering the hurtful words, the harsh tone. "He brought me to America because he needed an authentic Polish chef to cook for these people. One he could get cheaply. I made very little money. He charged me for my room at a very high price. And, he threatened to get my visa cancelled if I caused trouble. He vowed to not pay my way back to Poland. I would be homeless on the streets. I tried to find another job, secretly, but the restaurant owner across town where I applied called my godfather as a courtesy because he saw Lech Kaminski's name as my sponsor on my visa."

Luke cupped her shoulders, his touch was gentle, intimate. "Oh, Ania. He held you prisoner. Damn it, I hate that you had

to live through this for three years. Who does that to someone?"
He pulled her against him and hugged her. She rested her
cheek on her chest, closed her eyes. She inhaled his earthy,
clean scent. She felt the weight of his arms against her back. He
believed her. "What lead up to you almost marrying Dorek?"

She shook her head. *No. He could not know this.* He could
not know she was a witness to a cold-blooded murder when she
walked into the alley behind the restaurant to take out the
garbage and saw Dorek shoot his best friend. Nor could Luke
know that it was her godfather who hid her in the basement
from that night until the day she was taken to the wedding—all
to keep her from speaking to the police against Dorek.

She could not tell Luke all of this but she had to tell him
something. The truth. She couldn't lie to the man she loved any
more. But, she could not put him in more danger with the full
story.

"Dorek became obsessed with me," she began speaking the
truth. "He wanted to marry a Polish-Catholic woman. He liked
the way I looked. He liked that I had no male companions that
he ever witnessed. He liked that I could cook his meals. He
came to my room and threatened to take me to his bed often
but did not because his father had prevented it. Then, one day,
my godfather changed his mind. He said it was time for Dorek
to take a wife. My fate was sealed."

Luke extended his arms to hold her away to look at her.
She felt like he was looking into her soul. Did he see she didn't
tell him everything? It felt like he looked at her for hours, but it
was only seconds. Then, he nodded. Pulled her to him again.

"Ania, you're a threat to the bad guys," he said. "I know you
know that. You told me. But, you can't run from them forever.
You need to fight them on your terms."

She shook her head. "Luke, I am a person with no standing
in America. I am illegal. I have no visa, passport. I am on
overstay. How can I fight, if I can't even drive a car, get a hotel
room or earn a paycheck? I can't talk to the police. They will
arrest me. My word will mean nothing. And, the people you
call, bad guys, have friends everywhere."

"Are you aware that Dorek was charged with murder and is
out on bail?" A flash of lightning brightened the sky over the
black gulf.

"I know this. His mother told me."

"Is this all you know about the murder? What his mother
told you?"

She nodded, feeling sick to her stomach for lying to him.

He tugged on her hand. "Let's get back to the condo before it rains."

"Yes." Lightning flashed again, it still seemed far offshore, but with the dark sky and vast ocean, she didn't really know how far it was. "Luke. I promise to answer any questions you have...but, please, no more tonight. Let us enjoy our dinner. Rest. Enjoy this beautiful beach."

"Okay, Ania." He smiled, as the first fat drops of rain started to fall. He pulled her along faster. "A respite for tonight," he shouted as the rain grew louder. "But then we have to figure out how to stop throwing peas against the wall."

Chapter Eleven

Luke started to wake Ania before sunrise to walk on the beach. He knew she'd want to do that before they left for Cane, especially since last night's storm had washed a lot of seashells on shore. He changed his mind, though, as the peach glow of the early morning sky slipped through the open window and cast her naked flesh in a magical glow. *Let her rest another hour*, he thought, glad that he'd changed his mind about not making love to her the night before.

Like he had a choice.

Distancing himself from her and keeping their relationship friendly, sounded like a good idea in his head. But, he cared about what happened to her more than what was good for him and his business considering how complicated her world was. He enjoyed being with her on the cool sheets of his bed more than he should too. No, distance was not possible.

His guest room remained empty all night when she unintentionally seduced him over the dessert she called angel wings—*Chrusciki*. Damn, but watching her lick the powdered sugar off her lips after biting into the flaky, mouth-watering fried dough nearly dropped him to his knees. Before he knew it, his mouth was tasting her sweet mouth. No, he had no willpower to resist Ania. But, he had to.

He was torn. His heart believed she was telling him the truth, but his head feared she was not. Damn his father for crushing that part of him, leaving him unable to trust anyone fully—anyone except his sister.

Work. He would concentrate on his work, which always grounded him.

Luke turned on his computer, sat at the kitchen counter and checked emails, but they didn't hold his attention long. He began searching the Internet for Polish mobs in Atlanta; Dorek and Lech Kaminski; and Henryk. He researched immigration overstay, RICO cases and the restaurant where she'd worked. He stayed on the computer until Ania walked into the kitchen and he took her out onto the beach to collect shells. While they walked, he gathered his thoughts and formulated a new plan.

He thought of that plan as they drove toward Cane, too. It

was dependent on Ania agreeing to it. He'd wait until they reached New Orleans to tell her what it was.

"We're not going to stop in Fairhope, Alabama or anywhere else to take photos today," Luke said as they drove onto the Interstate causeway over the calm Mobile Bay with the city of Mobile's uncrowded skyline of skyscrapers ahead of them. It was a clear, sunny day, but he'd left the top up on his car. He wasn't in the mood to enjoy the last leg of their journey. Big changes were ahead of them in less than three hours.

"Please do not alter your work because of me," Ania said, her voice almost a plea. She played with the large, pink buttons on the dress Tanté Izzy had given her on that first day they had met. He understood she'd worn it because she'd be seeing Tanté Izzy later in the day. "I know you want photos of the shops and cafés in Fairhope. You told me it is beautiful how they are located in old Victorian homes and it is an inspiration how the shopping areas should be built in Magnolia Row."

"I'll return if my construction company gets the job."

"What is that?" Ania asked looking out the window off to their left. "Is that a military instillation?"

"No. It's the retired USS Alabama battleship. It's a memorial park open for visitors. Look next to it. That's a submarine."

She nodded and settled back into her seat, but she continued to look at the marsh grass, a lone fishing boat bobbing on the bay and the landmark seafood restaurants along the water's edge. There was no joy shining in her eyes.

Are you thinking about the end of our journey, Ania?

He knew he was.

"Luke. It is time to talk peas on the wall," she said, her hands now flat on her thighs.

"That's Mobile," he said, changing the subject. "It was once called the Paris of the south."

"I have been thinking..."

Nope, too soon to talk about what needed to be done. He didn't let her finish her sentence. "It's a little known fact, but Mobile was the first to have Mardi Gras."

She nodded. Inhaled deeply. "That's nice. I have something to tell you..."

"Save it." He pointed to the navigation screen. "We have about three hours to New Orleans...right there. We'll talk then. I don't want to spend our last leg arguing."

She nodded. "I do it for you, Luke."

He looked at her, the way her voice carried so much emotion when she'd said she'd *do it for him* and the way her eyes softened, made his heart skip. It felt like she was talking about something deeper, more meaningful than not having the conversation now.

"The phone," she said, touching him on the arm. Holy crap, he hadn't heard it ringing. "It is Tanté Izzy." She pointed to the car's monitor with her name on it.

"You talk to her." He answered the phone by pushing the button on his steering wheel.

"Mais, it took youz long enough to answer," she said, her heavy Cajun accent seemed heavier over the speaker. "I hope it'z because you took Ania to a good breakfast and dat's where youz are now."

"Hi Tanté Izzy. You are speaking to Ania."

"*Bon Matin.* How are you?"

"Good," She swallowed hard. "I saw the Gulf of Mexico and I harvested sea shells from the beach for you and Ruby."

"I love seashells." Tanté Izzy said, sounding sincere. "I got me a big bowl where I like to put them on my dresser."

"You would've needed a bigger bowl, if I hadn't stopped her from collecting all those seashells," Luke said, laughing.

"Babcia, I went for a swim into the Gulf of Mexico, too" she laughed.

Luke smiled thinking of her racing in to the water, diving head first into a wave, fully clothed. She was so totally free of burdens when she did that. She was happy. He wished she could always be just that way. A wish was a waste of time. So was the guilt he felt. But damn it, he had both.

"It felt wonderful," she laughed. "How are you, Tanté Izzy?"

"*Tres bien.* Very good. I'm happy youz comin' today. Luke tole me you like home cookin' so I'm cookin' a Cajun shrimp fricassee for you."

"Sounds wonderful. I cooked *Chruscki* for desert, too. I hope you like it."

"I know I did," Luke said, winking at Ania. Her cheeks turned a pretty pink.

"Cranky-crust?" Tanté Izzy said after several tries to pronounce the desert name.

"Close enough," Luke laughed.

"What time can I expect y'all?"

Ania looked at Luke. "It's nine now," Luke said, thinking

about the stop he planned in New Orleans. "Around one. If we're running late, we'll call you."

"I have good news to tell you in person, Ania."

She looked at Luke. Her expression said she was surprised that it was possible to receive any good news.

"I gotz you room ready," Tanté Izzy continued, her voice light, happy. "It'z in my house, youz know. It faces da bayou."

"Prepare a room for me too," Luke said. No way was he going to let Ania and Tanté Izzy stay in the house without him there to protect them.

"Harrumph. A please would be polite, youz know?"

"Please."

Two hours later, they were on Decatur Street in the New Orleans French Quarter. He'd purposely driven here to pass in front of the iconic double spire, St. Louis Cathedral, knowing Ania would love to see the landmark Catholic Church in the Crescent City before heading downtown. He was glad he did. She had her nose pressed to the window, like a child looking at the first snow.

"I feel like I am in Europe," she said, her voice sounding the most excited he'd heard it since leaving Orange Beach. "The architecture is very French, no?" She didn't wait for him to answer. She rushed on. "Yes, maybe Spain, too. The town square in front of the cathedral is like we have in Poland. It has much green grass and trees. And, pink azaleas." She leaned forward to look up out the window. "How special those balconies are on those red brick buildings around the square. The metal along the front looks like black lace."

"That's the Pontalba apartments. And that's Jackson Square between them." He said, driving at a snail's pace in front of it so she could take it all in. "Look closely on the wrought iron. There's an **A and P monogram on the grillwork. That represents the maiden and the married names of the Baroness who had these apartments built—Almonester and Pontalba."**

A horn blew behind him and he sped up, crossed over Canal Street into downtown. He reached Poydras Street and parked along the side of the street. Ania unbuckled her seat belt so she could fully turn to face him.

"Please do not interrupt me this time," she said, looking directly in his eyes. "First, I must say, with all my being, that I thank you. Thank you for showing me this special, historic city. Thank you for giving me experience with many, many beautiful places, but," her voice caught and she looked away toward the traffic passing in the busy street. Luke started to speak, but she faced him again, placed her finger over his lips and shook her head. "Please, let me speak." She looked at him waiting for him to agree. He nodded, but he didn't want to hear her thank him anymore. Not when he was about to break her heart.

He was doing the right thing, yet he felt like a son-of-a-bitch doing it. He'd always worried about being hurt by a female equivalent of a selfish bastard like his father. Now, in the name of doing what was right, he was going to be a heart-crushing bastard like his father. Ania, smiled a tight smile and kissed him on the cheek. A stab to his heart wouldn't have hurt more.

"Thank you for taking me out of Atlanta. You saved my life. And, doing that, you enriched it." A tear slid down her cheek. "In a very strange situation, I have been the happiest I have been in my life, even while I was the most scared. I do not know how you made me laugh so much, when I was one step away from sleeping homeless in a dark hiding place. You gave me purpose with the job and a little hope. No other man would have done this. No one."

Each word she spoke turned that painful knife in his heart a little more. "Ania, it wasn't me. You're a survivor. You're going to get out of this mess. I promise." He hugged her for a minute, running his hand over her long silky hair, as he looked over her shoulders to the big white building behind her.

His decision was made. He couldn't do it.

He looked at Ania. Then, he started the car and drove away from the United States Eastern District Office and the US Attorney's office.

"Buckle up. It's time to get to Cane."

Chapter Twelve

"This place seems very secure," Ania said, as they drove up to the locked gate for Sugar Mill Plantation and the Sugar Mill Plantation Kennel. A tall, white fence connected to each side of large gate blocked the driveway. This fence Luke had just explained, was designed to prevent the dogs in Ben and Elli Bienvenu's care from escaping or being stolen. She looked around them as they waited to be buzzed onto the property. "There are kilometers and kilometers of sugar cane crops around here. Are they sugar cane farmers too?"

"They lease some of their land to a farmer, so they don't actually farm it themselves." Luke said, looking at the emails on his phone.

Ania looked behind them to the thick sugar cane fields across the highway they'd just exited. There wasn't a farmhouse or any house there. She actually had only seen one farm on their drive down the two lane highway. It was very different than how it was in Poland. She opened her window to allow the light breeze outside to flow in her window and out Luke's window that he'd opened to press the gate's call button. The air was warm, damp and clean. It carried the fresh, familiar scents that reminded her of home—dark, rich soil heated by the early afternoon sun and sweet, healthy, plants swaying in the breeze. A rush of grief gripped her heart as she remembered how happily her parents used to sing along with the radio as they worked in the organic Bintje potato fields on their farm in Gordziko. They always had that radio with them. Clothes, a few photos, the medal she wore on her wrist, and that radio were the only possessions she had carried with her to America. She wondered if her godfather had tossed her prized possessions into the trash when she'd left.

Luke glanced at her and smiled. Even though she felt sad over the memory, and was nervous about meeting Tanté Izzy and Ruby's family, his smile calmed her a little.

"I wish Tanté Izzy hadn't asked us to come here," she admitted. "I would have liked to be with just her and Ruby. This is...well, very much."

Luke squeezed her hand. "Ania, I asked them to move the lunch here. I have many reasons for doing this. It's in your best interest." The buzzer sounded and the gate swung open. "Trust me on this. I'll explain later." He drove through the gate and it immediately closed behind them.

"Why would you do that?"

"Trust me."

She sat silently, as they passed three small weathered, but well-maintained cabins on one side of the road and a large barn-like building on the left surrounded by a fenced pasture. Five dogs darted over piles of timber, brick and smashed cars in what looked like a training exercise with the four trainers who were giving them hand signals to guide them through the debris. The dogs, trainers and landscape did not distract her from what Luke had just said. Every cell in her body wanted to push him to explain why he wanted to move the lunch to the plantation and why he did so without discussing it with her first.

"I will not continue to ask you for the reasons of this decision," she began, her anxiety making her heart pound hard in her chest, "only because you've asked me not to and I will respect that for now. But, I ask you to respect me and not make any more decisions that involve me. Ever. I do not like or want decisions to be made on my behalf. Do you understand that?"

"I understand, Ania." He blew out a breath. The road narrowed and a small river-like waterway he'd called a bayou earlier, flowed alongside of them. "But you have to know that I will do what needs to be done to protect you. Sometimes that means I have to do it without asking you first."

There was both comfort and frustration in hearing him say that. "You must remember; you are not the boss of me."

Luke started laughing.

"What? Did I say that wrong?"

"No. You said it exactly right." He pointed toward the bayou where an alligator moved slowly out of the brown water near tall, thick grass. "I bet you don't have those in Poland."

"Good Lord, no." She shook her head. "Although a frozen crocodile was found in the Masury forest once. Alligators and crocodiles are different, no?"

"Yes." Before he could explain the difference, the road curved toward a sugar cane field of young green stalks in the sable colored earth. The huge Sugar Mill Plantation came into view in front of them.

"There she is. Isn't she a beaut?" He stopped the car to look at the grand plantation home from a distance.

"She is stunning." Ania loved the way he spoke of buildings and homes as if they were a living person.

"Aguste Francois Bienvenu, who constructed this home in 1870, put a lot of thought into it. And though it has been added to over the years, each family member who did, maintained the spirit of the original design." Ania noticed how his eyes looked like new stars in the night sky and his voice flowed like a song as he spoke of the home. She enjoyed hearing and seeing him speak of the old planation more than looking at it. "You see the way the back of the plantation has almost a farmhouse-style with the back porches on both the lower and upper floors? It is meant to look and function for casual family use. To feel like a comfortable home."

He pointed to the back entrance. Ania, didn't look to where he was pointing. She had spotted six vehicles parked nearby, adjacent to a large barn. Her stomach knotted. That was a lot of vehicles. That meant there were at least six people inside that she would be meeting soon. Would they welcome her? Would they think she was a fool for running away with Luke, a stranger? Did they know of the danger she was in?

"The oldest part of the house is the center segment," Luke continued, unaware of the nerves tying her stomach in knots. "It's the original part of the home. It has simple construction with white-painted cypress planks under a clay-tiled roof. The additions on both sides of the main home, with the curved walls and large windows, there, with the green copper roof, is Victorian style. That was the style about forty years after the original home was built."

"I like the oak trees behind it. Their branches hang heavy, like long arms from the very big body. Like a giant in the green field."

"You'll love the front, if you love the oaks here." He smiled, turning to look at her. He studied her eyes a moment, gently touching her cheek. "You will love the Bienvenu family too. They're kind and fun-loving. Caring."

"Tell me more about the house." She wasn't ready to go in just yet even if he was right about this family.

"You can't see the front of the home from here. She faces the bayou and is very formal and regal from that side. There are double rows of oak and cypress trees that form a canopy over the walkway. Very stately.

"Does it have a balcony too?"

"Yes. A veranda on the lower level and matching balcony upstairs. It spans the entire home. There are heavy, square French style columns providing the structural support and creating the grand feeling of Sugar Mill Plantation. My favorite part is the twelve wooden casement windows lining the front of the home from floor to ceiling. They are wide enough for two people to walk through side by side, but they open traditionally with a sliding sash.

The back door opened. "Tanté Izzy." Ania clapped her hands together and laughed. "She is wearing the exact dress that I am wearing. That is so funny."

She waved to them to come inside and Ania felt a strange mix of nerves and excitement. This woman she barely knew, made her feel as she did when visiting her Babcia. It was magic and love. It made her think of special hugs, cabinets filled with her favorite treats and the scents that were only at Babcia's house. Despite her worries at meeting the Bienvenus, she opened the car door and rushed toward Tanté Izzy, not waiting for Luke to drive closer and park next to the other cars.

Tanté Izzy came down the final steps and opened her arms to her. Ania walked into her hug, enjoying this quirky old lady's scents of powdering make-up, drug-store hair spray and sweet vanilla perfume.

"Bout time youz got here."

Ania felt the sting of tears, but held them back. "Yes. Bout time."

Tanté Izzy, released her and gazed at her head to toe. "Glad to see Luke's been treatin' youz well. You look happier, healthier, since I last saw you."

"He is a very good man." She looked toward the screened door, where she could hear the voices of people laughing inside.

"They'ze good people inside, too."

Luke walked up to them carrying the bag filled with Chruscki and gave Tanté Izzy a kiss on her cheek. "I got her to you in one piece."

"I never doubted dat." She rolled her eyes. "And, I see she gotz you back in one piece too. Dat's good because you weren't when I saw you last."

"Huh?"

"Let's go inside."

Ania grabbed Luke's hand as she walked inside and held on tight. She wasn't sure when it happened, but she had come to rely on him.

As expected, the Bienvenu clan was a friendly group. What Ania hadn't expected was how comfortable she would feel with them. They were a lively, loud and energetic family, but she never felt crowded or imposed upon by them. They simply said hello, introduced themselves to her and then acted as if they were longtime friends. The conversations did not focus on her running away from her wedding, or anything about her really. They spoke about the crawfish fricassee Tanté Izzy prepared, her deserts which they ate with enthusiasm, the dogs weaving between their legs and the other normal things family spoke about.

Some of their accents were hard to understand in mass, Ania admitted, but when she spoke to Ruby and her very Cajun husband, Big John, there were no language barriers. Even Ben, who was soft spoken and had an easy southern manner, was easy to talk to, along with his wife Elli, who showed her the latest school photo of their seven-year old son, Joey. As owners of the plantation she would have expected Elli and Ben to act as host and hostess, but everyone wandered through the kitchen, opening drawers and cabinets at will, as if it was their home too. She supposed it was, considering as Ruby explained, most of the Bienvenu men had spent much of their childhood there.

"Jackson spent the least amount of time here," Ruby said, as they watched him tease his brother, Beau. Beau had just pulled his fiancé, Jewell, on his lap and gave her a gentle kiss on the cheek.

Ania had a longing to have Luke kiss her in that tender, fun-loving way. Would she ever have that? How could she when the man she loved would be on a different continent?

"Come sit by me," Mignon, Jewell's grandmother said, pointing to an empty chair at the large roughhewn table. She looked to be about at least five years older than Tanté Izzy. Her granddaughter, who stood to take the seat on the opposite side of Ania looked up at her and smiled.

"Please join us," she said.

She had avoided going anywhere near the table because Jackson and Beau's father had been there. As soon as she walked into the busy kitchen, she spotted him and went on alert. He was wearing a dark gray, police uniform. Although she had been introduced to him, and in a friendly manner he told her to call him by his first name, Ronald; she did not trust him. Maybe it wasn't fair, since he did not act threatening in any way, yet, she feared what he could do to her all the same.

"You need this," Mignon said, her accent very different than the Cajun French accent Tanté Izzy had. When she spoke to her grand-daughter as she tugged to remove a white plastic ring with a yellow stone shaped flower on top, she realized why. Her native language was a formal French.

"She wants you to have this ring," Jewell said, her eyes were twinkling as she helped her grandmother take the costume ring from her arthritic finger. Once removed, she handed it to Mignon.

"Take it." Mignon reached for Ania's hand and slid the ring on her marriage finger. It was too big. "You don't have a ring. All married women should have a ring."

Jewell's eyes widened and she looked at Beau who was still sitting in the chair a few feet away. The room seemed to quiet for a moment, then Ruby said something, that Ania couldn't hear, and everyone started laughing.

"I'm not married. But thank you for offering it," Ania said, placing the ring into Mignon's palm.

"*No les mariés?*" Mignon asked Tanté Izzy as she walked up to the table. "I thought you said she was married."

"Not me. Uh-uh. No sirree." She squeezed her mouth tight and shook her head.

"It must be the old-timers," Mignon told Ania, frowning. "Hell of thing to not remember so well. My Jewell and Beau are very patient with me even though I forget a lot." She sighed and Ania's heart melted. "Take the ring anyway. You don't have any jewelry except for the medal on the ribbon at your wrist. You're too pretty to have naked hands."

Ania took the plastic ring, slid it on her right hand. "Thank you." She kissed Mignon on the cheek. "It's beautiful."

"Let me see that?" Beau said, reaching over the table to take Ania's hand in his. "Mimi, I think you gave this young lady the prettiest of all your rings." He released her hand and Mignon nodded, a smile on her face. By the smile on Beau's face, Ania understood they had a special connection. She glanced at Ronald, who was smiling too. The deep lines from the corner of his eyes told her that he smiled often. Like both of his sons. Suddenly, she wasn't quite as afraid of him as she had been.

She glanced at the silver star on his uniform shirt. He tapped his finger on the star and Ania realized she had been staring at it. "Every little boy's dream to wear one of these," he laughed, easily. "I don't know if Luke told you, but I'm sheriff of this parish."

She shook her head and didn't meet his eyes. "I did not know."

"He's planning to retire soon," Ruby said. She pointed to Beau. "And, that one there, he's going to be the next sheriff. Mark my words."

"From your mouth to the voters' ears," Beau laughed.

"Hell, I hope she's right," Jackson laughed, leaning against the cabinets near the sink. "Otherwise, who's going to fix my speeding tickets."

"*Alohrs pas*. Like he's going to do dat. He's as honest as his papa. He might give you *extra* community service work if you get'z youzelf too many speeding tickets–just because youz is his brother."

"And, here I thought having a brother as Sheriff was going to come with some perks," Jackson teased, shrugging his shoulders.

"He makes da misère dat one," Tanté Izzy said pointing to Jackson.

"He makes too much trouble," Jewell interpreted again. "Mischief."

Despite her worry over the Sheriff, Ania found herself laughing with everyone else. Ania looked at Luke who was laughing too. When his eyes met hers, bright and focused on her, the room seemed to slide away. He gave her a slight knowing nod that they had connected in the midst of all the people around them. But, that connection was broken just as quickly as it came. He looked away as he removed his phone from its clip and read a text. As he did, his eyes darkened and his jaw tightened.

"I've got to take care of some business, Ania," Luke said, squatting next to her chair a few moments later. "I hope you don't mind staying here with Tanté Izzy, Ruby, and most of the others." He glanced at Beau and Ronald, who stood and walked over to Jackson.

"Can't I come with you?" Ania asked Luke, feeling there was more to them leaving then they were telling her.

He shook his head. "I won't be long." He kissed her on the forehead as he stood.

Tanté Izzy walked up to Ania and took her hand. "Remember I tole youz about da good news. Well, I want to take youz to it," she said. "Go away, Luke. We gotz our own business to take care of."

Ania looked at Luke, her heart thudding in her chest. It was the first time in over a week that they were going to be apart. A cold shiver raced through her body. He bent down and whispered in her ear, and even his warm breath did nothing to abate the chill.

"You'll be safe here. Ben and Big John are staying behind with y'all." Then he mouthed the words, *trust me.*

Chapter Thirteen

Tanté Izzy and Ruby led Ania up the stairs. The sound of the happy chatter faded as they walked into an office to the left of the second floor landing. The room, with its fourteen feet high ceilings was bright and sunny from the natural light shining through one of those very tall windows Luke had described to her. But, it wasn't the extra-large window or the beautiful view of an oak tree's canopy that grabbed her attention. It was her wedding gown and veil. Both were hanging from the window frame on a padded pale pink hanger with tiny white pearls. The gown and long veil were bright white, pressed and without a single tear on it.

"Oh, it looks as perfect and not as overly fussy as it did the day of..." Ania didn't finish her sentence. There was no need to. "Do you think it will sell fast online?"

"Faster than you think," Ruby said, smiling. "We took some photos of it outside on the balcony, with those majestic oaks and cypresses in the background. We selected the one that looked most like a bridal magazine photo, put it online with details of the designer from the label and bam." She clapped her hands and then threw up her arms. "Da-dah we had three hits."

"It turned into a biddin' war for dat dress." Tanté Izzy ran her hand across the laced hem of the cathedral train. "We just put it up to see what would happen online just for kicks and giggles," Ruby added. "We thought we should sell it for you at The Second Chance Consignment store that Elli, Jewell and Abby own downtown. At least there, we could really market it for you." Ruby shrugged and smiled. "No need. It is sold. I hope you don't mind."

Oh my Lord! "Of course not. Thank you so much." Ania hugged Tanté Izzy, then Ruby. "I told you to sell it without the repairs that you made. You have made it much better. How much did it sell for?

"Two thousand dollars!" Ruby and Tanté Izzy shouted at the same time.

Ania plopped down into the office chair. Her head felt light.

That was enough money for a flight back to Poland. Now, she just had to get a passport, or let ICE arrest her and put her on the plane.

"When will we get the money?" Ania thought about how much money she owed Luke for the clothes and incidentals he had bought her. She just did not believe that clothes, a toothbrush and personal items should be included in their employment agreement. She would accept him paying for her hotel rooms and food, but not personal items. The problem was that with the cost of the plane ticket, there would not be enough to pay him back and give these ladies something for their trouble. She would pay them all back, even though she knew they would not want to accept it. Pride and a need to control this bit of her life would not allow her to have it any other way.

"Today," Ruby said, a huge smile on her face. "The woman who bought it said she lives only a few hours away from Cane. She'll meet us at the consignment store at four." Ruby looked at Tanté Izzy. "That's in forty-five minutes. Elli and Mignon will meet us there after they pick up Joey. Jewell will let us in the store. She and Elli want to give you a free shopping spree in the store."

Ania shook her head and stood. "Nie. I have enough clothes. I could not owe...I mean take any more."

"Don't be a *coullion*. Dis store is exactly dere to help women who are down on dere luck." Tanté Izzy stood in front of her. Ania couldn't help but smile at the image they must've made both wearing the same exact dress, one almost a foot taller than the other and sixty years younger. "And, cheré, youz is down on your luck." She winked at her. "But, not fer long. Let me get my purse so we can go get youz your money."

"Luke wants me to stay here at the plantation." Ruby and Tanté Izzy looked at each other.

"We can go to meet her," Ruby said to Tanté Izzy.

"Can we call the her to meet us at the front gate?" Ania asked.

"Let me try to reach her," Ruby said, sitting in front of the computer. She went to the site where they sold the gown and sent a message to the buyer. After five minutes she looked at Ania. "She's probably on her way to the store already. She might not be able to get these messages on her phone. I know I don't have that kind of thing set up on mine." Ania looked over Ruby's shoulder at the computer monitor. "If we don't show up with the dress, she might not come back for it later. She really seemed anxious to buy it, too. She might need it right away. We'll be banned from this site forever if we fail to sell our item to this highest bidder. That isn't important." Ruby waved her hand in dismissal. "We can sell it in Cane at the consignment store."

"Two thousand dollars is a good fee, yes?" Ania looked at the women. "Can we get that amount in the consignment store? I fear not because this gown is of a very particular style that does not appeal to many, I think. And, how many people would want it in my size too? We may not get another chance like this."

"That is true, but Luke wants you to stay here," Ruby said, shaking her head.

"He wants me to be safe," she told the women looking at her for a decision. "Ruby, do you think your husband would come with us into town? He can be our protector."

"Mais, I can protect you too," Tanté Izzy said.

***

Thirty minutes later Ania, along with Jewell, Tante Izzy, Ruby and Big John walked inside the prettiest secondhand store she had ever seen. It was obvious that there was still a lot of work to be done before the store opened for business, but the décor that was already up and way it was painted told her that it was going to be a very lovely place.

"Your store is as trendy and beautiful as the finest boutiques in Warsaw," she told Jewell who walked past the three fashionably dressed mannequins wearing different plaid jackets over brightly colored striped yoga pants, to walk to a pair of soft cream colored upholstered chairs near the front show case. Jewell, as Ania had discovered less than a half-hour before, was an antiquities expert with a PHD, who enjoyed restoring old furniture.

"Thank you, Ania," she said, smiling. "Do you like the color of these chairs? Tante Izzy thinks they are too boring."

Ania laughed. Of course she did. Not only did the sweet, elderly woman wear clothes as vivid as her personality, she owned a truck that was just as colorful. Ben who had come along with them, remained outside in Tanté Izzy's bubble-gum pink classic American truck. It was so unusual how no one had acted like that bright old truck was a strange thing, although Ania was certain there wasn't another like it anywhere else in the world. Even now, Ben, who had driven the ladies in the truck as Big John followed in his SUV, was neither embarrassed nor bothered to sit inside of it to speak to a client who had called him about one of the dogs he had trained for a fire department.

"I think the color is very classic and beautiful," Ania said, looking up at the brightly painted purple, orange and yellow chairs hanging along the walls above a single acrylic shelf with black shoes on it. "Yet, so are those," she pointed to the chairs almost looking like they were defying gravity and floating there. "Those are classic 1970's, no?"

"Not really, but the intent was to mimic the mod colors that were indicative of that decade. They are actually just some old wooden chairs I found on the side of the road."

"Such vision," Ania said in awe of Jewell's talents. What else has she transformed in the store? She looked to the back where there were iron and upholstered bed frames, stacked in front of silver and blue silk curtains. The placement was clever, intriguing and inviting for a shopper to explore.

"Jewell has gotten a lot of the furniture ready for the store early because she is also preparing for her wedding in a month," Ruby said, walking around a stack of boxes in the middle of the store. "Elli and her friend, Abby, who lives in Hollywood, will get the clothes, shoes and accessories portion of the store set up before the grand opening. These women are so talented and are doing a good thing here – raising money with the sale of the merchandise to help women in need of finding their Second Chance."

Ania nodded. Yes. It was a very, very good thing they were doing. Too bad there was nothing in the boxes yet to unpack that could help with her immigration problems.

"Big John," Ruby shouted in a tone that was both loud and full of humor. "I can't believe you are already snoring." She rolled her eyes. "Look at him all comfy spread out on that leather chaise."

"Youz better hope he doesn't drool and getz dat pretty dark burgundy leather all spotty," Tante Izzy said, opening a box next to her and pulling out a bright red, silk scarf. She wrapped it around her neck before reaching into the box again to do the same with a canary yellow and peacock blue scarf.

The door opened and Jewell turned. "We're not open for business, yet," she began, walking toward the front of the store. Ania didn't hear what she said next, as she spotted a stack of books on the floor past the jewelry case. A hand written sheet of paper rested on top of it...*Cookbooks!*

Single mindedly focused, she rushed to them, anxious to see what was there. Her godfather had a few cookbooks in his office off of the kitchen at the restaurant, and she read each one, cover-to-cover at least a half dozen times. They were all filled with Polish recipes, except one. The *Joy of Cooking*. It was her favorite, knowing that Julia Childs had learned to cook using it. She wondered if there was a copy of the *Joy of Cooking* here. Maybe, she could buy her very own copy. Before she looked for it among the cookbooks there, a very thick Louisiana Cajun Cookbook by Chef John Folse captured her attention.

"I'm here to see someone about a wedding gown."

Ania gasped as the voice in the front of the store pierced through her mind like a sharp knife. She dropped the heavy cookbook and rushed behind a nearby bookcase. It was Dorek. She didn't have to see him to recognize his deep, lazy, oily voice. She felt like throwing up.

Run away!

She turned toward the back of the store where she knew there had to be an exit. But, she didn't move. She couldn't leave everyone there with him. Dorek would use them to get to her. If it meant he had to hurt them or kill them, he would do it. Oh God. What to do now? She thought about the rifle hanging against the back window of Tanté Izzy's truck. It was too far. And, she couldn't alert the others in the store that the man there would harm them. If she did, he would certainly hurt them to protect himself and to get her.

To get her. Yes. He had to get her to protect himself.

She stepped out from behind the bookcase. "Hello Dorek," she said, her voice sounding stronger than it should with the way her knees and hands were shaking.

"Ania."

The front door opened. Ben walked inside and leaned against the door. Dorek glanced at him and smiled the most menacing smile she had ever seen. More menacing even than the smile she had witnessed on his face the second after he had killed a man who had been his best friend for his entire life in the alley behind his father's restaurant. He would have no problem killing her and everyone in the store now.

She should not have run. It just made it worse. She had put these people she cared about in danger.

"Bodyguards, Ania?" he asked in English, taking a step closer to her. She heard Big John breathing from where he stood very close behind her. She wanted to tell him to go away, not to threaten Dorek. He was very dangerous.

But she said nothing. She didn't want to say the wrong thing to bring his wrath down on them faster, harder than he might otherwise. She sucked in a breath as nerves and fear made her mouth and throat so dry that her lips stuck together. She had to do something to get Dorek away before he hurt these kind people. She held her head high, looked directly into his dark, evil eyes and spoke to him in Polish. *"Your father will not approve,"* she said, knowing that might not be true. *"He swore before God that he would take care of me if my parents could not. You know this. He honors his vow."*

"My father is not here," he said in Polish, then in English he said, "You dishonored him when you ran away from our wedding. You dishonored me. And, you dishonored these people when you ran away with them."

"Speak for youzelf," Tanté Izzy said and Ania took a step forward toward her wanting to put her body between Dorek and this very special person. As she moved, Jewell moved toward the register where there was a phone sitting on the counter.

Dorek held up his hand for Ania to stop moving, and tapped his waist to let her know he was armed. Ben took a step further into the store. He motioned Tanté Izzy and Ruby to get down.

What happened next, seemed to happen in slow motion and maybe it did, because Tanté Izzy's old body didn't move that fast. She shouted, "Don't move mister or youz is goin' to make my day," as she pulled a long barrel revolver from the royal blue purse she wore on her arm.

Dorek turned, laughing, and drew his weapon as the front door burst open and two of his men charged inside the store. Two more of his men came rushing from the back of the store. She knew all four of them and shouted their names to stop and not hurt anyone. It was futile. Ben threw a punch at Dawid, who was closest to him as Josef hit Ben over the head with his gun. Tanté Izzy fired her weapon, hitting Dorek in the lower leg. Blood exploded like a breached dam over his jeans as he dropped to his knees.

Ania rushed to Tanté Izzy and pulled her behind the counter, near Jewell, knocking her to the floor. Ruby screamed a second before there was a heavy thump against the wooden floor.

"John. My John," she shouted.

Ania hadn't heard another gunshot, so she was relatively certain Big John had been hit on the head like Ben.

Jewell looked at her from where she was crouched on the floor near her. Her pretty, kind face was bright red. She pointed towards the phone near the register. Ania shook her head no. It was too dangerous for her to reach for it. Tanté Izzy, squirming against Ania, lifted her gun over her head and pointed it toward the front door. "I'm goin' to either shoot me a bad guy or get us some attention from the café across the street. Cover youz ears", she shouted and Ania had barely got her hands over her ears before Tanté Izzy pulled the trigger. Glass shattered. Josef cursed as some of it hit him in the face. Blood rolled down over his eyes and down his cheek.

"Get Ania," Dorek shouted and footsteps started pounding toward them.

"Come near Ania and youz are goin' to get a bullet in your man parts," Tanté Izzy said, coming up to her knees. She didn't wait for them to get any closer when she fired at Dawid who was the first to move toward Ania. He hit the ground, grabbing his thigh. "Next time, I'll aim for what I said I would," she shouted. "Youz will wish Lorena Bobbitt had gotten to you instead of me."

Had any of these men near them been Dorek, Tanté Izzy would be dead. Thank God, Josef and Dawid seemed to have a problem gunning down a little old lady, and Dorek was still on the floor bleeding.

Through the busted front door, sirens screamed in the distance. Dorek cursed as he struggled to his feet. "Let's get the hell out of here," he yelled as Josef hooked an arm around his waist and helped him hobble toward the back door. They left Dawid bleeding on the floor near the glass case no more than three steps from Jewell. Ben still laid face down, motionless, another five steps away from them. The other man who had come with Dorek, Michael, was already gone.

And Dorek would be too.

She had to stop him. Ania yanked Tanté Izzy's gun from her hand. She'd had enough of Dorek and the evil things he did. She didn't want to wait in fear for him to come back to get her...to get her friends.

Friends.

Yes, she had friends now and she would protect them.

"*Stop, Dorek,*" she said in Polish, walking around the front case and pointing the gun at the back of his retreating head. "*No more. Enough.*" Then in English she said, "It ends now."

"Ania, no," Ruby shouted. "Let him go. The police will get him."

Dorek turned and faced Ania, his weapon drawn. "Get the car started, Josef," he said in English. "She's right. It ends now." Josef looked at Ania. There was something in the way his eyes met hers that made her think he was considering coming to her rescue. But, then he turned and ran out the back of the store.

"Tsk. Tsk. Tsk." Dorek said, perspiration dripping along the side of his wide face. He winced as he took a step toward Ania. She cocked the hammer of the gun as she had seen done on television. God, she hoped she was doing it right. He laughed, then spoke to her in English again. "Is this any way to treat your fiancé?"

"You're not her fiancé." Luke said as he walked up behind Dorek and pressed the barrel of his gun against the back of Dorek's head. Ania kept her weapon pointed at him, too. "Drop you gun."

Dorek laughed and dropped the gun. Luke kicked it far away from everyone. "This is not over. I have friends."

"All whom are being rounded up as we speak by the FBI and being charged with racketeering, organized crime, and being dumb asses," Luke said, pressing the weapon harder against his head. "On your knees." He shoved Dorek down and the man grunted from the pain from where Tanté Izzy had shot him.

The Sheriff walked in, blood dripping from his mouth. "We got the others," he told Luke, wiping the back of hand over his injured lip. "They put up a fight, but they're headed to lock-up now. EMT just drove up." Ronald handcuffed Dorek as his deputies did the same with Dawid, then waved the EMT's in and they started to help the injured, including Dawid and Dorek each guarded by two deputies.

The sound of a car's tires screeching outside had everyone stopping. Dear Lord, was it coming through the building? A second later, Beau came running into the store. "Jewell," he shouted, his voice sounding as wild as he looked. "Jewell!"

"Here," she cried, just to his left, behind the boxes where Ben had fallen. She had the cell phone in her hand. She stood, and the paramedic tending to Ben nodded for her to go on, not that anything he had said would have stopped Beau reached out and lifted her into his arms. She buried her face into his chest, and he closed his eyes. "Thank God you are all right."

Ania looked at Luke then, his breathing was so heavy and fast...or was that hers? He holstered his gun at the small of his back, and walked to her. "You can put the weapon down, sweetheart," he said, his voice gentle. She looked at him and started shaking. He took the gun from her hand and handed it to the Sheriff who had walked up to them.

"I thought we all were going to get dead," she said, her voice trembling. He wrapped his arms around her and pulled her against his chest. Relief flooded her body first with warm gratitude then with an icy fear. She began to shake.

"Are you injured?" He looked at her from head to toe and after she reassured him she was unharmed for the third time. Still he had the EMTs check her. When they said she was fine, just a little shaken up, Luke gathered her in his arms again. "You could've been killed," he said, sounding both angry and concerned at the same time.

She pushed away from him. "You could have been killed. All of you." Her voice caught in her throat. She looked around the store at the people who were hurt, bleeding and concerned about their loved ones.

Ruby was at her husband's side, pressing her blouse against the back of his head where he was bleeding, as the paramedic was reaching into his medical bag assuring her he was going to be fine. Tanté Izzy was on her knees helping Dawid and lecturing him about changing jobs.

"I did this to them. I brought this here." Her body was shaking violently now. She couldn't stop it. "I am so very sorry." Luke lifted her into his arms and carried her to the lounge chair in the back of the room. He must have taken a jacket off one of the racks they passed, because he was putting it over her shoulders now.

"Just take deep breaths Ania." He began rubbing her arms, trying to warm her.

"This was Dorek's fault not yours. If you are going to play the hindsight guessing game, you should blame me, too. I'm the one who brought you to Cane."

"You told me to stay at the plantation. I did not listen."

"When Ben called to say you were here and the man I had showed him a photo of was here, I..."

"I came here to sell my gown," she interrupted, her head spinning with the adrenaline that was still rushing through her body. "I was a fool. All I thought about was that I was to get enough money to go back to Poland, to pay..."

"Poland?" Luke shook his head, then pulled the edges of the jacket together over her chest. "Do you really want to go back to Poland, Ania?"

She nodded, but her heart screamed, *No!* She wanted to stay here because she loved Luke and wanted to be with him. She wanted to stay because she had made good friends with some very kind and caring people in the short time since she had run from her old life. *But, what did you bring to them to make their life better?* She looked at Ruby whose face was streaked with tears as she spoke to her husband. *Only bad.* Ania turned to look into Luke's eyes that were steady on hers. What did she give him that made his life better? *Nothing.* Only problems when he had a big job to do to save his company.

Love and friendship was not a reason to destroy good people's lives. It was a reason to leave them. Besides, Luke did not love her back. If he did as she loved him, he would be struggling for each breath he took, knowing they would soon be apart—as she was.

He released her hands. "Okay, then let's clear your name and get you back to Poland."

She nodded again, unable to speak while her heart was shattering.

"I've come up with a plan to help you. Jen, Jackson, Beau and others have been working all morning to make it happen." He sat on the lounge next to her. "You have a couple of options. First, I have a solid solution to keep ICE from arresting you for overstaying your visa and deporting you. It will keep you from having a blemish on your record that could prevent you from traveling abroad again, and at the very least complicate it. I'll explain that in a minute."

He looked away, as if he was gathering his thoughts. Ania saw the muscle in his jaw tighten. She had learned in their time together that meant he was upset. She wanted to comfort him, but fought every cell in her body to do so. They were not on a journey together anymore where they had made love in Alabama with the Gulf of Mexico waves crashing outside their windows; where they had laughed until their eyes teared at an onion festival in Glenville, Georgia; and where they had worked side-by-side in unpracticed synchronization in a hotel room in

Washington, Georgia. They were two people who had come to the end of a road trip together and were preparing to move on with their lives.

"You have another concern to deal with," Luke continued, his voice even and steady, unaware of her sadness. "The feds. They want you to testify against Dorek and his associates for murder and for the RICO charges filed against them today."

"RICO?" She had no idea what that was but assumed it was bad if the United States government was involved.

"Organized crime. Your godfather and his cronies were involved in some bad stuff." She nodded. "Jen got the US attorney to agree to let you do a videotaped testimony, through the DA and sheriff's office here in Cane. We can have it certified by a local judge. When it's time for the court hearing, if the defense wants to cross-examine you, they can either fly you back to Atlanta or set up a video-conference call to Poland."

"So you want me to go to Poland?"

"I didn't say that. Jen assumed you'd want to go back. And, she thought it might be what I wanted you to do, too."

She wanted to ask him if it was what he wanted, but she was a coward. What if he said yes? Besides, if his sister, who knew him best, thought that he wanted her to go back to Poland, he probably did.

"Jackson offered to represent you if you want him to be your attorney through all of this. He has a lot of experience with international and federal law from his years in Navy JAG." He puffed up his cheeks and blew out a breath. "If you stay, you don't have to do a videotaped testimony, but Jackson can still be your attorney."

"That is very kind of him."

"That leaves immigration." He stared at her a long time before speaking again. "I have that worked out, too. You have options."

"Thank you," she whispered, her heart feeling like it was shattering.

"Jackson thinks he can negotiate a deal with the US Attorney's office to get the overstay visa cleared. He can maybe do something before ICE comes to arrest you. The process will overall take some time with them–paperwork and processing is not a speedy thing with the government. You'd have to deal with the Polish Consulate too. The closest one is in Washington, DC." He smiled. "Not Washington, Georgia." His smile slowly faded. "Do you want to wait, Ania for the bureaucratic process?

Because if you don't, I have a faster solution. It is a fast-track. It's really simple." He paused and looked into her eyes. "You marry me."

Marry him?

Not a real marriage. A marriage of convenience to get her back to Poland faster. He'd asked her if that was what she wanted, but was it what he wanted?

She leaned forward. "Even if I wanted to do this, for convenience, I cannot marry you without identification. I would still need to travel to a Polish Consulate to get proper identification or to Atlanta to see if my passport has not been destroyed, which I think it was since Dorek planned to get me dead." She shook her head. "Are you sure you are uninjured? You are talking with no sense. I cannot have documentation by tomorrow to marry. The government will not recognize it as legal without it and you will be in trouble for attempting it. I have put you in enough problems."

"Ah, but there is a way in Louisiana." He shifted to face her better. "I called a priest friend here in Cane who helped me figure this part out. We discovered there is a Louisiana Napoleonic Code that says that the church documents are equal to legal state binding documents. And, we discovered that in Catholic Canon Law paragraphs a bishop can allow a priest to marry a couple secretly if a prior inquiry was made to the couple's readiness for marriage and there are two witnesses are present for the ceremony."

"First, what is Napoleonic code?" She tucked her hands in the side pockets of the jacket.

"It's the legal code we use in Louisiana," Luke explained carefully. "When Louisiana became a state in 1812, it adopted the former French and Spanish codes used in the colonies to govern. This is the version of the Napoleonic Code that we mostly use here today."

"So a marriage can happen with no identification?"

"Not exactly." He paused as the paramedics rolled Dorek and Dawid out on stretchers. Ben and Big John laughed at something Tanté Izzy said as they were standing at the front of the store on unsteady legs. "The Catholic church requires proof that you were baptized. And, they require the local bishop to sign off on the unconventional marriage."

"You got my baptismal certificate from my church in Gordziko?"

"I did." He motioned to Tanté Izzy who had walked up to

them. "This well-connected lady got the bishop to sign off on the speedy marriage."

"Ruby gotz da flowers for da church and fer youz to carry down da aisle," she added. "And a weddin' cake."

"After the wedding, we'd file for an *immediate relative green-card*." Her head felt like it was spinning. "Even with an overstay visa, this is possible and relatively uncomplicated to do. Ania, it will take much less time to get through the immigration process if you are married to an American citizen...to me."

Marry Luke. To get through the immigration process faster. Not to marry for love. It sounded awful. And, illegal. What did he gain by marrying her and doing this for her?

"Why Luke? Why do you offer to do this for me?

"Because I care about you. You deserve your freedom...your happiness."

"It is against the law."

"Only if this is a fraudulent marriage," Luke's eyes softened. "This will be a legal marriage.

Legal. It did not appeal to her the way he stated it. Yet, if she did it, there was a path for her to be done with this confusing, awful, wonderful part of her life.

"So, Ania, if you agree to it, we can be married at ten tomorrow morning. What do you say?"

She sucked in a breath hoping to settle her trembling body. She looked deeply into Luke's eyes and then answered. "*Nie.*"

Chapter Fourteen

Ania had said, *no.*

It nearly brought him to his knees. He hadn't realized just how badly he wanted to marry her. And, if he was honest with himself, it had nothing to do with her getting getting deported. He wanted to marry her because he cared about her. Care. Hell, it was more than that.

He loved Ania.

He'd fallen in love with her the afternoon at the Atlanta Botanical Gardens as she swung over the colorful cloud of blooming flowers on a wooden swing.

Why hadn't he realized it when he was talking about marriage yesterday? Damn it. He was so hell bent on sticking to his plan that he couldn't see what was right in front of him. The plan—marry an American—him, so she could return to Poland legally on a faster track, just as she wanted. Job accomplished. His stupid pride would be intact. It was bull-shit. The plan was for him to marry her so she could go instead of what it should be, to marry her so she could stay.

Luke looked at his watch. It was ten minutes before he was scheduled to marry Ania. Even after she had said no, he'd told her he would be waiting for her at the church, to marry her. All she had to do was show up. Which, he hoped she would do once she had a chance to think it through and realize marriage was her best option in dealing with her illegal immigration status. As he looked toward the church door, willing it to open with her standing there, he just wasn't sure she'd come to that conclusion.

Then what in the hell would he do?

His best friend and best man, Hunter James, was talking to the priest and giving Luke the space he needed to stew over where Ania would show up or not. *Would she? Or was she going to be so stubborn that she'd not marry him and let the ICE agent standing in the back of church arrest her where she was staying at Tanté Izzy's house?* Then she'd have to start the process with Jackson that he'd outlined for her.

Marry me instead, Ania.

The back door opened, a bright bar of sunshine slid down the center of the church, before it was cut off when the door was closed again. Tanté Izzy walked forward and the twenty-something people waiting in the pews looked down the aisle toward her.

Luke's heart stopped beating. Crap. She was there to tell him Ania wasn't coming. Tanté Izzy waved her hand in huge arc for him to come to her. He sucked in breath and walked down the aisle. Best get this over with.

"Ania wants to talk to you," she whispered when he reached her. He nodded and swallowed hard. "She's outside in my truck." Tanté Izzy handed him her keys. "I took the keys; in case she wants to be a runaway bride again."

He tucked the keys into his pants pocket, thinking if she wants to get away, he wouldn't fight her on it. He had pride, and he wasn't a fool.

Luke opened the driver's side door to Tanté Izzy's truck and climbed inside. He looked at Ania. She was wearing a pretty, short white dress with a thin trim of white lace along the scooped neckline and bottom hem. Around her neck on a sheer white ribbon was the medal her mother had given her. "You look beautiful, Ania. Breathtaking."

She smiled. "You do too. That black suit is very handsome."

"It's a tuxedo," he said, feeling shy and nervous. If she was wearing a white dress, with her hair pulled up on top of her head with soft curls, maybe...maybe she would marry him. "You wanted to talk to me?"

"I do." She shifted in her seat and he noticed that her neck and cheeks were flushed. "Luke, I do not know if I will say the correct words with my nerves so high."

"Just talk to me. Like you did when we were on our road trip."

"Yes." She nodded. This past week with you, traveling around the south, working by your side, disagreeing on subjects, sharing new experiences and. . . .making love to you, I've come to decide something. I must say it or forever have regret."

Luke turned completely in the seat to face her. When he did, the large steering wheel dug into his ribs, still sore from fighting with Dorek. He winced. Ania's brows narrowed together. He realized by the way her beautiful, pink lips turned down, she thought his expression of pain was because of what she had said.

"Ania, I had a great time with you too. The best."

"Really?"

"Yes, really."

She opened the passenger door and got out of the truck. Luke didn't allow himself to feel the pain that was scratching at his heart as he watched her—not run away, as he feared—but instead, walk around the car to his side. What was she doing? She opened his door. Luke eased around to face her. His heart started to thud so hard in his chest, he thought Ania must be able to hear it.

She dropped on one knee. Luke sucked in a breath. "Luke, I do not want to marry you just because of ICE."

"If you don't want to marry me, why are you down on a knee?"

"I am saying this wrong." Luke climbed fully out of the cab of the truck and went down on one knee too. He took her hands into his.

"I don't want to marry you because of ICE either."

She smiled and removed her hands from his before reaching into the top of her dress to retrieve the white, plastic ring with the dull yellow stone flower on top of it that Mignon had given her. "Will you marry me for love, Luke?"

She was proposing to him!

"I will marry you for love," Luke said, his throat tight with emotion. She slipped the ring on his ring finger, but it only fit to his second knuckle.

He leaned forward and kissed her gently on the mouth. "I love you, Ania."

"And, I love you." Tears slid down her cheek. Luke drew her up with him and hugged her as they stood.

The church doors flew open. Tanté Izzy stood with the ICE agent as she shouted to Luke and Ania. "*Mon Dieu*, are y'all comin' in to get *maire* or not?"

"*Let's go tie the knot*," Luke said to Ania enjoying her wide-eyed, happy expression.

"That is an idiom that puts me on cloud nine."

Luke scooped her up and carried her to the church.

Coming Summer of 2017!

Abby,
A Second Chance Novel
by
Tina DeSalvo

Abby McCord is the daughter and granddaughter of beloved silver screen legends, but has not followed in their footsteps. Yet, because she's considered Hollywood royalty, she was thrust into the public eye from birth. Something she has tried to avoid in her adult life. She can't escape it any longer. She's the prime suspect of a highly-publicized theft of the non-profit foundation that she founded with her best friend, Elli Bienvenu. Hunted by the paparazzi and fired from her job, she accepts her best friend's invitation come to the small, quiet town of Cane, Louisiana to stay in a private cabin at the Sugar Mill Plantation.

Jackson Bienvenu, freshly retired as Navy JAG is working on an important project in his hometown. The deadline is nearing and there is still much to do. At the urging of his family, he hires Abby–a former, high-powered, L.A. attorney with skills and a whole lot of problems. It's even more than he initially understood when the paparazzi finds her and the LAPD begin to tighten their case against her. Now, not only does he have to get his project completed, but Jackson finds himself working to find out who the "real" thief, who is setting up Abby and threatening her life is.

From Chapter One...

...Abby kicked her shoes aside and walked to the door barefoot. "Come on in, Tanté Izzy," Abby said, opening the door. "We can't have the damp night air ruining your beautiful hair. I'm sorry. It's just..." Abby's voice trailed off.

Tanté Izzy wasn't alone.

A tall, broad-shouldered man wearing a black, well-tailored tuxedo stood next to her. He also wore a smile and black rain boots with bright green alligators on them.

"Are youz goin' to just stand dere wit youz pretty robin blue eyes poppin' out youz head or youz goin' to let us come in?" Tanté Izzy didn't wait for a response, she walked into the cabin. "Oh *mon Dieu*. Youz act like youz looking at an ax murderer. Youz know my nephew, Jackson. He's da best man in da weddin'. Beau's brother."

Ax murderer? Had she really said that? Were her earlier thoughts that obvious in her expression? God, she hoped they couldn't see how upset she was over the detective's earlier call too. She really didn't have her parents' polished acting skills. Abby forced herself to relax and let go of the door that she held in a white-knuckle grip.

Jackson. He was still smiling, his bright sea-green eyes filled with humor.

"We haven't officially met, Tanté Izzy," he said, his voice deep, smooth, and with a hint of a Cajun accent. "But Abby and I did have an encounter. I remember it clearly. I'd never forget that very distinctive voice of hers speaking to you via Facetime during Elli and Ben's wedding."

His last comment snapped Abby out of whatever stupor she'd fallen into at the shock of seeing someone with Tanté Izzy. "Dear Lord, was I so loud that you could hear me during the wedding ceremony? I thought I had fixed all of the settings before I mailed Tanté Izzy the iPad to use."

Jackson turned his hands up and shrugged. "I think Tanté Izzy cranked the volume all the way up."

"Well, that's embarrassing." She may have over-estimated Tanté Izzy's abilities to use the iPad. To Abby's great disappointment, all she'd gotten to see of her best friend's wedding were close-ups of Jackson's mouth, bow tie, and right ear, along with the distant shots of the church's popcorn ceiling and Tanté Izzy's pink bonnet.

"I found it...amusing." Jackson smiled again, and she remembered seeing that same smile during Elli's wedding.

Her stomach knotted and her heart pounded fast in her chest as she suddenly had a strong urge to knock that smile off of his face and walk away. Why was she reacting to him this way? Why did he put her in such a defensive mode? It wasn't like he actually was an ax murderer, or reporter, or anyone who could be a threat to her. He wasn't a total stranger.

In fact, his smile seemed to be so genuine that it made his beautiful light green eyes appear friendly. He did have a strong jaw, dark military-cut hair, straight posture, and two scars-one above his right eyebrow and the other at the corner of his lips. Those things didn't make him a threat nor frightful. It made him look strong, capable, and formidable. Like the late-thirties-year-old retired military man he was.

No, he wasn't a scary stranger. She knew a little about him. Jackson Bienvenu was a retired Navy JAG. A lawyer like herself, or he had been before he retired. She didn't know what he did now. Elli hadn't mentioned his name in a long time. They'd spoken of Jewell's wedding, the consignment store, the foundation, and the foundation thefts. Not Jackson.

No, he didn't feel threatening. He just felt...dangerous.

That was insane. Jackson was part of Elli and Tanté Izzy's family and someone they both adored. Still, dangerous was the word that kept coming to mind. Perhaps it was just a lingering thought from the LAPD phone call. Or, maybe it had more to do with that strange video-call encounter they'd had.

She remembered it well; it had been about a year ago. He'd been wearing a classic black tuxedo then too. She had seen a lot of his tux and the way he filled it out because Tanté Izzy had a hard time keeping the iPad pointed at Elli and Ben at the altar, which Abby had actually wanted to see since she couldn't be at her very best friend's wedding.

She still felt awful that she hadn't attended, but she had gotten a call that her father had had a heart attack as she was about to board the plane at LAX to travel to the wedding. She was told to rush to Cedars-Sinai Medical Center right away. It was bad, and she had to be with him and her mother.

"Abby, let me properly introduce myself, then you might allow me to come inside," he said, humor in his eyes. "I'm Jackson. Elli and Ben's cousin." He extended his hand and Abby shook it with a firm, single pump. His grip was confident and appropriate, yet it felt as intimate as if he had kissed her hand.

She cleared her throat and looked him directly in the eyes as much because it was proper to do so, as to challenge herself to prove she didn't really feel he was any kind of a threat. "Glad to meet you, Jackson." She stepped aside to allow him to join Tanté Izzy in the cabin.

Tanté Izzy stood in the center of the room, looking thin, petite, and adorable. Soft pink Mandevella was the color of the simple knit cardigan she wore over the same color satin gown with a rhinestone belt over her tiny round belly. Her chandelier rhinestone earrings swung to and fro as she walked up to the mirror above the antique walnut dresser. She pressed at the sides of her short fluffy curls as she glanced at Abby over her shoulder. "I think I'm goin' to have Margie give me a medium blond rinse so my hair is youz color. The color of sun on wheat. Hmm, maybe extensions too, so it's halfway down my back like you too."

Jackson's smile was huge now. He winked at Abby. "You're a trendsetter, Ms. McCord." He shifted and focused his attention on his aunt. "I think you're perfect the way you are, Tanté Izzy."

"*Mais,* I know dat." She waved a hand. "I just want me some pretty braids pulled back into a ponytail like Abby. She always got her sophisticated braids flowin' into the rest of her hairs that's not braided. I like dat me. It's real pretty."

Jackson looked directly at Abby. "She has a point."

Abby felt her cheeks heat.

About the Author

Tina DeSalvo, a fresh, humorous voice in romance, brings her knowledge and passion for the culture, traditions and people of Cajun Country (where she lives) and New Orleans (where she grew up) to her **Second Chance Novel** series-*Elli, Jewell* and *Abby* (coming this summer!). Tina is also a journalist who spent her career in television news and as one of the first female sports broadcasters in Louisiana. A Breast Cancer Survivor, Tina donates her proceeds from *Elli* to help individuals fight the disease. She loves to write, but she especially *loves* spending time with readers...sharing laughs, tears and hugs. Learn more about Tina at tinadesalvo.com

Proof

Manufactured by Amazon.com
Columbia, SC
06 April 2017